It was a perfect night...

When Brad had parked on the mountain, he came around to open Sarah's door, then took her hand and led her to the lone stone bench.

When they were seated, Sarah tried to withdraw her hand. But Brad held on to it. After a few minutes, he brought it to his lips.

"What are you doing?" she whispered.

"Kissing your hand."

"Why?"

"Because I like to." He kissed it again. "Because I think you're very sweet and thoughtful. And because I believe you're strong for your brother and sister, and so I want to be strong for you."

He kissed her palm this time, then up to her wrist.

If a gentle, harmless kiss like this could make her heart race and her mouth dry, Sarah wondered, what would a real kiss from Brad Logan do to her?

Step into a world where family counts,
men are true to their word—
and where romance always wins the day!

JUDY CHRISTENBERRY

has written more than seventy books
for Silhouette Books®, and she's a favorite
with readers. Now you can find Judy's
heartwarming and powerful stories in
Harlequin Romance®.

Don't miss her next books:

In this Harlequin American Romance story,
Judy revisits the Lazy L Ranch:
The Lazy L Saga: Jessie
Available in November

Indulge in the magic of Christmas in Judy's next
Harlequin Romance novel:
Cinderella and the Cowboy
Available in December

JUDY CHRISTENBERRY

The Rancher's Inherited Family

Western Weddings

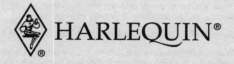

HARLEQUIN®

TORONTO • NEW YORK • LONDON
AMSTERDAM • PARIS • SYDNEY • HAMBURG
STOCKHOLM • ATHENS • TOKYO • MILAN • MADRID
PRAGUE • WARSAW • BUDAPEST • AUCKLAND

ISBN-13: 978-0-373-18385-2
ISBN-10:   0-373-18385-2

THE RANCHER'S INHERITED FAMILY

First North American Publication 2008.

www.eHarlequin.com

Printed in U.S.A.

Judy Christenberry has been writing romance fiction for fifteen years, because she loves happy endings as much as her readers do. A former French teacher, Judy now devotes herself to writing full-time. She hopes readers have as much fun reading her stories as she does writing them. She spends her spare time reading, watching her favorite sports teams and keeping track of her two daughters. Judy's a native Texan and lives in Dallas.

In the cowboy's arms...

Imagine a world where men are strong and true
to their word…and where romance always wins
the day! These rugged ranchers may seem
tough on the exterior, but they are about to
meet their match when they meet strong,
loving women to care for them!

If you love gorgeous cowboys and Western settings,
this miniseries is for you!

Look out for more stories in this miniseries,
only from Harlequin Romance®.

In September don't miss the next story
in the Western Weddings miniseries:
Texas Ranger Takes a Bride
by
Patricia Thayer

CHAPTER ONE

BRAD LOGAN was late.

He should have left his friend's wedding back in Pinedale hours ago, and now he was still twenty miles away from home. His brother would be angry if he woke up Abby. Though they had a couple months to go before being born, the twins in her belly were already not letting her sleep.

Because he was speeding by, Brad almost missed the flicker in the pasture to the left, a bit of land the Logans rented from the government. Braking to a stop, he backed up to see if it could be true. He thought everyone knew not to have a campfire on government land.

There it was, almost hidden behind a small hill. He had to snuff it out.

His headlights picked up tire tracks leading off the macadam. Following the tracks, he came upon a darkened old car and the offending campfire right beside it.

Only after parking his truck and walking up to the fire did he notice the young woman who sat beside it, obviously in deep thought.

"Ma'am?"

Startled, she jumped, losing her balance on the rock on which she sat. Getting up, she dusted off her rear, sputtering, "Wh-who are you?"

"The name's Brad Logan. My family rents this land from the government. You're not allowed to camp here. And you're definitely not allowed to have a campfire."

"We're not doing any harm."

"Lady, it's been a dry year. We can't take any risks of a forest fire. I'm sorry, but the fire has to go." He kicked dirt onto the fire, but the woman stopped him.

"If you knew how long it took me to get that fire started, you wouldn't so cavalierly destroy it!"

He shook off her hand. "Look, you don't even have any business being out here. We've had bears down this low. What would you do if a bear attacked you? You need to go back to Pinedale and get a motel room."

"No! No, I can't!" The woman appeared distraught.

"Why not?"

"I don't— Money is tight!"

"There's a campground at Yellowstone. I doubt they're crowded on an October night."

"Uh, yes, thank you."

Something in her face told him she wouldn't be going to Yellowstone, despite her verbal acceptance. Wherever she went, he couldn't leave her here.

"Do you have any water?"

"Yes." She turned toward her darkened car.

"I need it to be sure the fire is completely out."

Disbelief shone on her face when she spun on her heel. "You're going to pour it on the fire? I don't have much and the kids will need it in the morning."

His eyes darted around the car. "You've got kids here?"

She gave a brief nod, backing away from him. "Look, we'll go, but I need what water I have."

"Where are the kids?"

"They're sleeping."

"Lady, you need to do a better job raising your kids!"

"And you need to mind your own business!"

Not knowing what else to do, Brad took out his cell phone and called the sheriff. After filling him in, he asked, "Shall I bring her in?"

He was watching the woman as he spoke and when he mentioned taking her in, her eyes opened wide and she immediately began gathering the few things she had out. "We'll be on our way!"

Before she could reach her car, such as it was, Brad caught her arm. "The sheriff said for me to bring you in."

"But we haven't done anything!"

"Then you won't mind talking to the sheriff, will you?"

"Yes, I do mind. I don't want to leave the kids."

"Of course not. We'll take them with us…in my truck."

"No! I can't leave my car here!"

"If the sheriff says it's okay, I'll bring you back in the morning."

He walked over to the old car and looked through the window to see two kids sleeping in the two seats. "Where were you going to sleep?" he asked the woman.

"That's none of your business!"

He opened the car door, waking the children. "Hi, kids. Your mom has agreed to come to our ranch for the night. Is that okay with you?"

A small girl, maybe eight or nine, and a little boy who looked to be about five, the same age as his nephew Robbie, stared at him.

The children looked out for their mother, and he realized he'd never introduced himself. "Sorry, I forgot to tell you who I am. My name's Brad. We'll take my truck to the ranch. Okay?"

"Is that your truck?" the little boy

asked, getting on his knees and looking out the window.

"Yeah. Do you like trucks?"

He nodded. "I can ride in yours?"

"Sure. Ask your mom."

"But she's not here."

Brad turned to look at the young woman. "She's not your mother?"

"No," the little boy said sadly.

Just what the hell was happening here? Brad wondered. Not wanting to upset the boy, he said calmly, "Well, buddy, why don't you come ride with me? She'll follow us."

"Will you come, Sarah?"

"Yes, Davy, I'll follow you. I'm not leaving you behind."

The little girl got out of the car and moved to Sarah's side. "Sarah, I don't think you should let Davy go with him. We don't know him."

She put her arm around the girl and smiled. "It's all right, Anna. We're going to follow right behind."

Then the woman moved closer to Brad and whispered, "Don't even think of trying to take Davy from me."

"I won't, as long as you follow me."

She moved away from him and hugged the boy. Then she and the girl got in the old car and started the engine.

Brad helped the little boy into his truck and fastened the seat belt for him. "Davy, I'm glad you're going to ride with me. I don't like riding alone."

"Me, neither."

"Okay, we'll be home in twenty minutes."

But after five minutes, he noticed the woman—Sarah—wasn't behind him. He made a U-turn and found her car dead on the side of the road. "Davy, I need to see if I can help her. Sit here."

When he got to the car, Sarah had tears running down her cheeks.

"Are you okay?" he asked.

Quickly she wiped her tears away. "I'm fine."

"Do you know what's wrong with your car?"

"No."

"Okay, why don't you and Anna come get in my truck with Davy. We'll see what we can do about your car tomorrow."

"We—we need our suitcases."

"Where are they?"

"In the trunk. I'll get them."

Despite her independence, Brad retrieved the two suitcases from the trunk and put them in his truck.

"Here, Anna, let me help you up," Brad said to the little girl. Then he turned to the young woman, but Sarah had already climbed up into the backseat.

"Put your seat belts on," he directed as he got behind the wheel. "We'll be at the ranch in a few minutes." He pulled out onto the highway.

None of his three passengers responded. The children looked like they'd gone to sleep, but he could see Sarah watching his reflection in the rearview. When his eyes met hers on the mirror, she diverted her gaze.

She looked to be in her early twenties, with light brown hair that framed her face and fell to her shoulders. Her eyes were big, though in the dark he couldn't detect a color. Under ordinary circumstances, Brad suspected it would be a beautiful face, but right now worry and tension had painted dark circles under her eyes and tightened her mouth.

He wanted to ask Sarah who the children were to her, and why they were in her care, but he gave her her way and was silent for the rest of the ride.

When he got to the house, he turned to her with an arm across the seat and said, "My sister-in-law is seven months pregnant with twins. She has trouble getting back to sleep if she wakes up, so I'd appreciate it if you're quiet."

Sarah got out of the truck and helped Anna down. Then she opened Davy's door and helped the little boy.

"What are we doing here?" the woman asked. "I thought you were taking me to talk to the sheriff."

He'd taken her to the Logan ranch, his home. The sheriff, who happened to be his mother's second husband, had agreed to meet him there.

"This is my family's ranch. The sheriff's meeting us here. That's his car."

At the mention of the sheriff, her face seemed to blanch. "Are you all right?"

Her eyes, when she looked at him, were dark brown. "We didn't do anything wrong."

For some reason he felt compelled to reassure her. Maybe it was the way she obviously cared for the children, or because he'd discovered a soft spot for damsels in distress. Either way, he motioned with his hand for her to follow him.

He opened the door to the kitchen and allowed Sarah and the children to enter. The sheriff was sitting at the big oak table. "Mike, this is Sarah, Anna and Davy."

Mike stood. In his early fifties and with gray hair, he still cut a formidable figure. "Hello. I'm Mike Dunleavy, the County Sheriff. Have a seat. Would you like some coffee?" He nodded toward the counter, where he'd obviously put on a fresh pot as soon as Brad had called.

"No, thanks. But c-could the kids have some milk?" Sarah asked, as if asking a big favor.

Brad spoke up. "Of course. I'll get it."

After he had delivered the two glasses to the children, Mike began his questioning. He started with her name.

"Sarah Brownly."

"Are you on vacation?" he asked Sarah.

She pressed her lips together. Then she said, "Sort of. I lost my job and—and we decided to move."

"And those are your only bags? Your only belongings?"

She kept her gaze lowered. "Yes."

"Are these your children?"

Again she hesitated. Only this time it seemed minutes had passed before she finally shook her head.

"Where are their parents?"

"Anna and Davy are my half siblings. Our mother died recently."

Mike raised his brows. "I'm sorry," he said in a gentler tone. "It must be hard for you. For all of you."

Sitting across from her, Brad saw the tears form in her eyes. If she was lying, she was a damn good actress.

The little boy, who'd been quietly sitting, drinking his milk, slid from his chair and tugged on her sleeve. "I'm sleepy, Sarah."

She took Davy into her lap. Anna scooted

her chair close to Sarah and leaned against her, too.

Again Brad was struck by the tenderness that Sarah displayed toward the children. He couldn't help but feel sorry for the kids. "Davy, my nephew is about your age. He has an extra bed in his room upstairs. Would you like to sleep in it?"

Davy looked up at Sarah for permission. When she nodded, he asked Brad, "Won't he mind?"

"I doubt he'll wake up before morning. Come on. I'll show you." Brad led the little boy to the bedroom.

At the open door, Davy hesitated. "I think I want to go back to Sarah."

"Why don't you just lie down for a little while? Sarah's going to be fine."

After a moment's deliberation, the comfy bed won out. Davy climbed up into it and settled under the blanket. He glanced over at Robbie, still sound asleep in his own bed.

"Does he have a mommy?" Davy asked, pointing at the boy.

Brad nodded. "Uh-huh. My sister-in-law, Abby. She's asleep in another room with her husband, Nick. He's my older brother. He's in charge of this ranch."

The boy considered his reply. Then said, "My mommy's in heaven. My daddy killed her. He's in Denver."

Though he spoke the words quietly, they struck Brad with the force of a warrior. He had to hold onto the bedpost to keep from reeling back. Scores of questions assailed him, but he knew now was not the time to voice them. If what he said was true, this little boy had been through enough. He deserved to sleep like an angel. Sarah could answer the questions.

When Brad came back to the kitchen, he heard Sarah pleading with Mike to let her and her half siblings go. She promised she wouldn't camp out anymore.

Brad couldn't wait. He cut her off and blurted, "Davy said his dad killed his mom."

Sarah's face drained of color and he thought she was going to faint. He stepped closer.

"Is that true, Sarah?" Mike asked, watching her carefully.

This time she couldn't hold back the tears. Anna put her arms around Sarah, both of them hanging on to each other. "Yes," Sarah whispered.

"Did you report the murder?" the sheriff asked.

"Yes." After a moment, she continued, "The kids and I had gone to the grocery store. When I started bringing the groceries into the kitchen, I saw my stepfather choking my mother. I grabbed a chair and broke it over his head. I pulled him off Mom, but—but I couldn't help her." She choked back a sob, no doubt seeing the scene once again in her mind's eye. "He was out...my stepfather. I got the kids back in the car and I threw some things into our suitcases and left. Then I called the police and told them that my stepfather had choked my mother to death."

"Why did you run?"

"Because my stepfather is—he lies. I couldn't leave without the kids. He'd kill any of us if he thought we knew what he'd done. He wasn't a good father. I paid most of the bills and bought the groceries. He drank what little he earned. He had even started my mother drinking." At that confession, Sarah cried again. "I tried to get her to not drink with him. He was a fighter when he drank and she... She was a different person."

"I still don't understand why you ran off. You'd already called the police."

"Sheriff, have you come across people who do bad things but aren't punished for them? Because no one can prove it? Or because he tells a sad story and is let off easy? I couldn't risk hanging around to see what happened. He would claim he loved his children and the cops would believe him."

Mike seemed to ponder that, then he nodded, as if he'd understood her as well as agreed with her. "Look, why don't you and the children sleep here tonight? The Logans won't mind, right, Brad?" He looked up at Brad, who nodded his agreement. "I need the names of your mother and stepfather."

"Alice and Ellis Ashton."

"Let me contact the police in— You never said where you lived."

"I don't think I should tell you." She was trembling, but her chin was strong, as if determined to keep their former whereabouts a secret.

"I believe Davy said it was Denver," Brad said softly.

Sarah jumped to her feet. "You had no right to question Davy!" she protested. "He's just a little boy!"

"I wasn't questioning him. He volunteered the information."

Mike put up his hands to still the argument. "Sarah, we're not trying to harm you or your siblings. We're just trying to find out what happened. Believe it or not, we want to protect you." Once Sarah settled down a bit, he continued. "Do you have papers giving you the right to remove your brother and sister from their home?"

"If he gets the kids, he won't take care of them! He might—might even hurt them!"

At that, Anna began crying, and Brad questioned their judgment in speaking so candidly in front of the young girl.

Sarah picked her up and held her tightly. "Please, Sheriff! You can understand! I couldn't help my mother anymore, but—but don't let him take the kids!"

"Sarah, are you over twenty-one?" Mike asked.

"Yes, I'm twenty-four." She wiped her cheeks, but the tears kept coming.

"If you have to go back to testify against your stepfather, I'll try to help you get custody of the children. I can write a letter to the judge in support of that action. We'll keep the kids here if you go testify. If they don't give you custody, I'll—I'll look away for a day or two so you can disappear. Okay?"

"You promise?" she asked.

"You have my word."

"Thank you, Sheriff. They're good kids."

"I can tell that." He smiled at Anna. "Everything's going to be fine," he crooned to the little girl. "No need to cry."

Brad thanked Mike. "Is that all you need for tonight? I think Anna is pretty tired, too."

"Yeah, that's all for tonight. I'll check with the Denver PD to see if they've got an Ellis Ashton in custody."

"Then, Sarah, if you're ready, we've got an empty bedroom for you two to share tonight. Want me to carry Anna?"

"No, thank you. I'll carry her."

Brad picked up the suitcases and led the way down the dimly lit hall. He opened the farthest bedroom door and turned on the bedside light. "There are extra pillows and a quilt in the closet, in case you get cold during the night." He told her where to find the bathroom and fresh hand towels. All the while Sarah just stood there, holding Anna. She looked frozen to the spot, almost shell-shocked. He couldn't even imagine what she'd been through, how awful it must have been, how terrified she was. An urge to reach out to her and wrap her in his arms suddenly overtook him, hard and strong. He took a step toward her, but she backed up.

Looking at him, her brown eyes red-rimmed and bloodshot, she shook her head, but said in a small voice, "Thank you, Brad. Thank you for helping us."

* * *

Brad rose the next morning and showered and shaved, then dressed. After that, he headed for the kitchen, where he knew he'd find his brother cooking breakfast.

"Morning," he greeted Nick as he stepped into the doorway.

"Morning." Then Nick continued before Brad could say anything. "You got back kind of late last night, didn't you?"

"Yeah, but—"

Robbie raced into the kitchen, interrupting what Brad was going to say. Following him was Davy. "Daddy, look!"

Nick looked at his son and suddenly realized Robbie wasn't alone. "What the—"

"That's what I was going to tell you, Nick," Brad hurriedly said.

"He belongs to you?" Nick asked. "Something you forgot to mention, brother?"

"No, he's not mine, but I brought him here. I found him and his sisters camping out on the government land last night."

"That's not allowed," Nick said.

"I know that, but— Anyway, I put out

the fire and I brought them here to talk to Mike."

Brad was glad he got those words out because he heard more steps coming down the hall.

Sarah and Anna came into the kitchen. He noticed how much they looked alike, the same coloring and facial features.

"Good morning," Sarah said softly.

"Hello," Nick said. "I'm Nick Logan."

"I'm Sarah Brownly and this is Anna. And also Davy. If we're intruding—"

"Not at all. Have a seat. I'll have breakfast ready in a minute." Then he looked at Brad. "Can you get some silverware and drinks for our guests?"

"Sure." Brad got the silverware and poured three glasses of milk. After he brought those to the table, he filled a mug of coffee for Sarah and put it on the table. "Have a seat," he added.

Brad hoped Nick would not ask questions. He could explain the events while they rode after breakfast.

Nick didn't say anything until he'd dished up breakfast for everyone. But when he sat down to eat, he asked, "Where are you from?"

Sarah didn't want to tell him, but after a look at Brad, she replied, "Denver."

"It's an unusual month for a vacation with kids. Won't they be missing school?"

Sarah looked at Brad, a plea in her gaze.

"I'll explain after breakfast," Brad said. "Eat up, Sarah. Nick wants to get the kitchen clean before we go."

"I'll be glad to clean the dishes. I don't know what— I mean, I'll be waiting to hear from the sheriff."

Nick looked at Brad, as if wondering if he could trust Sarah.

Brad said, "That'd be good, Sarah, if you don't mind. The kids can watch cartoons while you work."

"Can I stay home and watch cartoons, too?" Robbie asked eagerly.

"No, son. You know you have to go to school. Mommy would be upset if you stayed home for no reason."

"Aw, Daddy. Why—"

"Eat up," Nick ordered.

They had all finished in a couple of

minutes. Nick took Robbie out to wait for his school bus, planning to meet Brad in the barn afterward.

As they left, Brad turned to Sarah. "My sister-in-law is sleeping in. Can you cook breakfast for her?"

"All right. Thank you for reassuring Nick without—without upsetting the kids."

"No problem," Brad said as he walked out of the house.

In the barn he saddled both horses and waited for his brother.

Minutes later he arrived, and he was barely in the saddle when he blurted, "Okay, what's the story?"

Nick might not have been prepared for the violent story, but Brad held nothing back. He told his brother as much as he knew.

In the end, Nick could only shake his head. "What a story."

"I know. And I only saw them because I caught a flicker of a fire. I stopped and went back. I put out the fire and told her she had to take the kids and leave. It was pretty obvious she thought she could just tell me she was leaving. I called Mike and he said to bring them in."

"She's lucky you found them," Nick said. "Been a shame if they'd made it away from the father and been attacked by the bears out there."

"That's what I told her."

But as Brad rode out beside his brother, he couldn't help wondering if he'd really brought Sarah to safety.

CHAPTER TWO

SARAH wondered if this ranch was as safe a place as the Logans and the sheriff had told her. She hated to think she'd led her brother and sister to more danger. After checking on them in the family room, where they were watching television, she returned to her kitchen chores.

She would've done a lot more work in return for the night's sleep at a good bed and breakfast. Lord knows she couldn't have gone without rest again. After running, she'd driven half the night and then parked in a rest stop to close her eyes for a few minutes, sitting up on watch for most of the first night. Then there was last night's fiasco in the national forest.

She hadn't thought about bears.

Thanks to Brad Logan, she and the children had been taken care of. A safe house, warm beds and good food. What more could she ask for? Sighing, she realized she owed Brad a lot. And to think she'd been angry at him when he barged in on her makeshift campsite last night. The sternness she'd seen in his eyes had softened to concern, then sympathy. She didn't want his sympathy, just his compassion. And the handsome cowboy had offered it.

After sweeping the kitchen floor, she heard footsteps coming down the hall. Her unknowing hostess, perhaps?

The brown-haired pregnant woman came through the door and stopped in her tracks when she saw Sarah. "Hello?"

"I'm Sarah. Your brother-in-law let us stay last night. May I fix you some breakfast?"

"No, I— Well, okay, if you don't mind."

"Of course not. There's still some hot coffee if you—"

"No, the doctor says I can't have coffee. I'll take a cup of tea, though, with milk and sugar in it."

Sarah not only fixed her the tea, but made toast, bacon and scrambled eggs. After she served the woman, she said, "I'm sorry if I startled you before—"

Abby held up a hand. "It's fine. I just wasn't expecting anyone to be here." She picked up her fork. "So, did you meet my husband this morning?"

"Yes, he cooked breakfast for all of us. I volunteered to clean the kitchen to repay him."

"That was nice of you. Do you want some coffee? It won't bother me, I promise."

"I'd love another cup. I was saving it for you." Sarah got up and poured the last cup of coffee and sat back down again.

"Are you a friend of Brad's?" Abby asked.

"No. We're—we're on the run from my stepfather. He—he killed my mother two nights ago. I was afraid he'd kill all three of us if we didn't get out of there."

Apparently Abby wasn't expecting such a gruesome story. She nearly dropped her teacup and her eyes flew to Sarah's. "Oh, no! I'm so sorry."

"Thank you," Sarah said, blinking rapidly to hide the tears that sprang to her eyes.

"You said we. Who are you with?"

"My two half siblings. They're watching TV in your family room."

"How old are they?"

"Five and nine."

"You certainly have your hands full, don't you?" Abby reached across the table and patted her arm, and the gesture was Sarah's undoing.

She broke down, releasing all the fear, anxiety and tension of the last few days in a flood of tears.

"These are good cookies."

Little Davy sat at the kitchen table munching on the homemade sweets that Kate, Abby's mother-in-law, had sent over. Even Anna seemed to like them, though she sat quietly.

After her breakdown, Sarah had brought the children in to meet their gracious hostess. Abby took to the children immediately.

"I'll tell her you like them," Abby said. "She's a wonderful grandmother to Robbie."

Sarah smiled. "I'm sure she is. Is he her only grandson until your babies are born?"

"Yes. Nick's the only married child of her brood." After a minute, Abby looked around the kitchen. "I probably need to think of something for lunch."

"I think you should just tell me what you want done."

"I can't ask you to do that!"

"Yes, you can. You know your husband doesn't want you risking your babies."

"Well, yes, but— Do you mind?"

"Of course not. Just tell me what you have in mind. I'll fix it."

As Sarah got up, the phone rang. She looked at Abby with a question in her eyes.

"Yes, please," Abby said with a smile.

Sarah answered the phone. "Logan Ranch."

"Is this Sarah?"

"Yes."

"This is Kate Dunleavy, Mike's wife."

"And Robbie's grandmother?"

"Exactly. You've learned all of us already, haven't you?"

Sarah said, "Do you want to talk to Abby?"

"Yes, please."

The telephone had a long cord and she carried the receiver to Abby.

While Abby was talking, Sarah took a quick inventory of what food they had on hand. The stocked cupboard and refrigerator were astounding for Sarah. She wasn't used to such abundance.

Abby said goodbye and Sarah was beside her to take the phone back to the wall.

"Kate's bringing over a casserole for lunch. We just need to cut up a salad."

"Okay." Sarah quickly got to work. Setting the table for six, she put the salad out and heated up some black-eyed peas. When Kate arrived, everything was ready.

"You did all this?" Kate asked. "Abby, you know you shouldn't. I was going to do the work."

"I didn't, Kate. Sarah did everything. Isn't she great?"

"She certainly is." She walked over to the newcomer and put out a hand in greeting. "Hello, Sarah. I'm glad to meet you."

The woman, who looked to be in her fifties, with graying light-brown hair, was so welcoming that Sarah returned her handshake. "I'll—I'll go call the kids."

Kate watched the young woman leave the room. "Mike says she's a good person."

"I think so, and she's had a horrible time of it. Does Mike think he can help her?"

"Yes, he thinks so. He'll tell her his news after we all eat. He doesn't want to talk in front of the children."

"Oh, of course—"

Sarah entered the kitchen, followed by Anna and Davy. Anna pressed closer to Sarah. Davy didn't seem too concerned.

"Kids, this is Kate, the cookie lady," Abby said.

"I like your cookies!" Davy said with a big smile, which Kate returned.

"I'm glad. It's nice to meet you, Davy. You, too, Anna."

"Come on, kids, sit down at the table."

"I like Robbie," Davy said, grinning.

Kate seemed thrilled. "Perfect," she said. "Maybe Mike's idea will work out."

Sarah's head snapped up. "What idea?"

Mike entered at that moment. "Hi. How's everyone doing?"

Sarah nodded to Mike, smiling a little. "We're fine."

"Good. I'm starved. Are you ready to eat?"

"You're always hungry," Kate teased her husband. But she held out a seat next to hers at the table.

Sarah could barely eat. She was too concerned about whatever idea the sheriff had come up with. She was grateful when the meal ended and she took her siblings back to the family room.

As soon as she entered the room, she turned to Mike. "Did they arrest him?"

Mike sighed. "Yeah, but you were right. Ashton told them he didn't know who killed his wife. He said he was knocked out and couldn't help his beloved wife."

"I told you he lied."

"And he wants to know what happened to his children."

Sarah's hand flew to her chest. "No! I told you. They can't go back to him."

Mike tried to calm her down. "I just told you what he said. However, the police did a thorough job. They're holding him in jail until he can make bail for $250,000. They're hoping he won't."

"Good."

"They also want to interview you."

"No!" She felt as if she were on a seesaw, up one minute, down the next with the type of news Mike delivered.

"Sarah, you remember what I said? I talked to the police about you being appointed guardian of Anna and Davy. They agreed to pursue that for you, if you'll come talk to them."

She blinked her eyes, staring at her hands, clenched tightly in front of her. "I—I can't!"

"I think Brad would go with you. I'm going to talk to him in a few minutes."

"Why would he do that?"

"Because you need someone with you, Sarah. It won't be an easy thing."

"I know—and what about the kids?"

"Well, I thought they might like to go to

school while they're here. I'll set it up. It will be hardest on Anna. Davy will have Robbie to go to school with."

"But I can't leave them! It would be too hard for them."

"It will be even harder if you don't get custody."

Abby took her hand. "We'll take care of them, Sarah."

"But you're supposed to rest," Sarah protested.

"If they're at school all day, I can rest."

The sheriff looked at Sarah. "You have to answer this question. Is it worth going to testify against Ellis Ashton? You'll get custody of the kids and keep them safe."

When he put it that way, Sarah knew there was really no choice. She drew in a deep breath and said, "I'll go. But I don't need to bother Brad. I can manage on my own."

The sheriff shook his head. "He's going with you, Sarah. It's part of the deal. Nick and Abby will take care of the kids and Brad will take care of you."

"I don't want him to take care of me! I can manage on my own."

"Why don't you want him to go?"

"The only man in my family killed my mother. Why would I want anything to do with any man?"

Mike drew a deep breath. "He's just escorting you, keeping you safe. So you can come back to your siblings."

"I—I don't know what—"

"I'm thinking you should leave Monday morning after the kids go to school."

"Their first day? No, that's impossible! Anna can't— She's very shy!"

"It's all right," Kate said. "I'll take her to school that morning and make sure she's happy. Abby will be here to help."

Sarah looked around the room at all the encouraging faces. "All right. I can tell her you'll go with her?"

"Of course."

Mike stood and kissed Kate goodbye and thanked Sarah for her cooperation. Then he left.

"Can you tell us what the children wear to school? Is there somewhere we can buy something for her to wear?"

"Yes. I can take you and Anna, and Davy, too, this afternoon, if you want."

"Thank you, Kate. I think it will help Anna feel good about herself." She just wished she knew how to pay for the clothes.

Nick and Brad came into the house for lunch a little later, only to find it empty.

"Where's Abby?" Nick mused out loud.

"I don't know. I guess we're on our own today."

"If she's gotten involved with those people you drug in, I'll—"

"Hi, boys," Mike called as he stepped into the kitchen. "Are the ladies out?"

"Yeah," Nick said in angry tones.

"Do you know where they are?"

"No. They didn't even leave a note." Nick couldn't believe his wife would disappear without leaving word of her plans. Not in her condition!

"Hey, here's a casserole I can warm up. I think there's enough for all three of us," Brad said.

"Ah, that's one of the casseroles Kate made," Mike said. "I'll set the table."

"How did you know about the casserole?" Nick asked.

"I had a quick lunch earlier with the ladies. But I didn't get enough to eat," Mike assured Nick and Brad.

Nick shrugged his shoulders. "Okay, I'll make us something to drink. Is coffee okay with both of you? I think the wind got colder today."

It wasn't until they were finished eating that Brad realized it was unusual for Mike to be out there during the day. He asked his reasons.

"I came to talk to Sarah," he explained.

"Why? Is something wrong?"

"No, not really, but I need some help."

Nick spoke up. "To do what?"

"To escort Sarah to Denver."

Neither man seemed upset.

"Who you gonna get?" Brad asked.

Mike just looked at him.

"Oh, no! Not me. Don't you have any deputies to handle the job?"

"You know I don't have as many deputies as I need to take care of the county. I can't send one of them away."

"But I think she'll feel better with a deputy."

"That's why I'm going to deputize you before you go," Mike assured him with a grin.

Sarah was sitting at the kitchen table that afternoon, trying to make sense of her life the past few days. Not that she was complaining. She seemed to have fallen into a good situation. Abby had offered her the job of housekeeper for at least three months at a generous rate plus room and board for all three of them.

Kate had taken them all shopping, even Abby, and she'd charged all the clothing for Anna and Davy, promising to take it out of Sarah's salary after she'd insisted. Sarah had bought more than she should, because the two kids had so little, but she didn't regret it. It was little compared to what they deserved.

All their lives Anna and Davy had suffered from their father's behavior. Even with Sarah living there and providing food, it wasn't enough. Children shouldn't have to live the way her siblings had.

The kitchen door opened and Brad walked in.

She jumped to her feet. "Do you need anything?"

Brad looked at her in surprise. "No, I was just going to get some water. The wind is cold at night, but the temperature is warm this afternoon. I was going to get a couple of bottles of cold water."

"I'll get them for you," Sarah said.

He stood there while she got the water.

"Uh, where did you go today? We didn't see anyone when we came in for a late lunch."

"But you found the leftover casserole, didn't you?"

"Yeah, Mike said Mom made it."

"Yes, she brought lunch for all of us. Did Mike eat lunch with you, too?"

"Yeah, you'd think he couldn't handle two lunches. I keep thinking it will catch up with him, but it never seems to."

After a second, Sarah got up enough

courage to ask if Mike had talked to him about going to Denver.

"Yeah, he mentioned it."

"Did you say yes?"

He looked at her then and she noticed the dark eyes with gold flecks that matched his dark brown hair, the lines at the corners of his eyes, no doubt from working outside on the ranch. He was a handsome man. A man's man.

A man she could fall for.

But she couldn't. Not now.

Before he could answer, she blurted, "I don't need you to go. I can manage on my own."

"You need an escort."

"It's ridiculous for you to leave your job to go with me. I'll be fine." She turned away from him and pretended to wipe the cabinet.

"I'm going. Mike's going to deputize me, so my presence will be official."

"There's no need."

"How big is Ellis Ashton?"

"Why?"

"I just wondered if he's scary."

"He's not quite as tall as you, but he's big enough around to make two of you."

"Hmm. I guess he could take me in a fight."

"Probably not. He's slow…and dumb."

Brad gave a half smile. "So, maybe I could take him?"

"Maybe. But it's neither here nor there. There will be no fighting!"

Brad shrugged his shoulders. "I was just thinking."

"Well, don't think. Just tell Mike no."

"Why don't you want me to go with you?"

"I don't know you! You're more of a stranger to me than my stepfather!" And what she did know—how good-looking he was—was a danger.

"Sarah, I'm going along to protect you."

"I can take care of myself."

"You want to compare muscles?" Brad asked with a grin.

"You're being silly!"

Brad turned serious. "Even if your step-father were a ninety-pound weakling, you need someone with you, to lend moral support if nothing else."

"I told Mike I could go alone. He's holding Anna and Davy as hostages! What more does he need to guarantee that I'm coming back?"

"Maybe he thinks you're planning on dumping your responsibilities and cutting loose."

Sarah immediately headed for the quickest exit.

"Why are you running away? Was I too close to the truth?"

She whirled around and charged back to him. "How dare you even insinuate that! Don't you ever say that to Davy and Anna!"

"Are you planning on coming back?"

"Yes! I won't dump Davy and Anna on your family! Unless—unless I can't come back," she said, ending in a whisper.

"Of course you'll come back. That's why I'm going. To make sure you do."

"If—if something happens to me, will Abby find a home for Davy and Anna? I know your family won't have room, but—

but maybe a nice family in the area? And keep them together?"

"Quit worrying about it, Sarah. You'll be back in a couple of days, and things will go on just like they've been doing."

"Abby hired me to be her housekeeper," Sarah informed him.

"That's good. You seem to do the work well."

"I guess. She's offering me too much money." She named the dollar amount.

"I guess Nick figured it in the budget. It's worth it if it keeps Abby from going into labor early."

"Yes. I'm grateful for the work…and for her taking in the kids. Kate said she would come over after school and fix them a snack and make a casserole that Nick could take out of the oven."

"That sounds like a good plan."

Sarah collapsed at the kitchen table. "I don't know what to do!" she exclaimed, covering her face with her hands.

Brad sat down beside her. "You do what Mike tells you to do. He's older and wiser. He won't steer you wrong."

"You have a lot of confidence in him, don't you?"

"He's married to my mother. We wouldn't have let her marry him if he wasn't a good guy."

She gave a bitter laugh. "You think you're always in control, don't you?"

"Most times. My family has lived here for over a hundred years, leaving me with a great tradition and enough money to make it."

She got up from the table and turned away from him.

"Yes, well, that's not our family."

"Why did your mother marry the man?" Brad asked, still sitting at the table.

"Alice was widowed and didn't have any job skills…and she had a teenage daughter—me."

"Did he drink then?"

"Yes, but he kept it under control. At least for a year or two. Then he'd just stop off for one beer that turned into four or five. He'd drag home about eight or nine and roar for his dinner."

"That sounds sad. I guess you didn't have much of a life then."

"No. I never knew if he'd come home drunk or not come home at all. It was embarrassing."

"When you moved back home, how old were the kids?"

"Anna was six and Davy was two." She'd had no choice, really, but to leave the city and move back in. Her own life wouldn't have been worth living if she knew her siblings were in danger.

Brad stood and moved to Sarah's side. "Don't worry, Sarah. Nick and Abby are going to take good care of your little family."

"They'd better!"

CHAPTER THREE

SARAH didn't want anything to go wrong with her first evening meal.

Heavenly aromas from her baking casserole gave her hope that the ingredients she'd found in the cupboards were perfectly blended. The peach cobbler cooling on the countertop could've been a magazine photo; she only hoped it tasted as good as it looked. The house was clean, the laundry done. The only thing left was passing muster. Muster being the approval of the Logans.

When she heard the men coming in, she felt her stomach flip. Nick came in first and then Brad. When they breathed the air, they came to an abrupt halt.

"Who's been cooking?" Nick asked. "If it's Abby, I'm going to let her have it."

Sarah turned from the counter. "It's not Abby. It's me. She's taking a nap. Do you want to wake her?"

Nick's expression relaxed and he left the kitchen to find his wife.

Brad looked at the perfectly set table and the cobbler and nodded in approval.

"Would you like some coffee?" she asked him, ripping her eyes from his tall, solid body, muscular arms and thighs.

"You've made coffee, too?"

"Yes, it just finished perking."

"Yeah, I'll take a cup."

"I don't know what exactly you want done every day. I should have asked you earlier, but if you'll tell me if I'm forgetting things, I can do them."

"Do you really know how to cook?"

"Yes."

Nick came into the room carrying Abby. He sat her down in a chair and teasingly said, "If those babies get any larger, I don't think I'll be able to carry you."

Sarah wasn't surprised when Abby burst into tears.

Nick, however, was startled. "What's wrong?"

Even Brad knew the problem. "Bro, you can't tell her she's too big. She's trying to bring two children into the world."

"No! Of course not!" Nick said at once. "I was just teasing, honey. You're doing fine!"

"Of course she is, Nick," Sarah said, coming to stand by Abby's chair. "And she hired me to be the housekeeper for three months so I can do what needs to be done and she can rest."

"Can you do those things?" Nick asked in surprise.

"You can let me know when I don't do things right."

Then she opened the oven and took out the casserole. It had browned to perfection. She brought the casserole to the table, then went to call Robbie and her siblings.

In a few minutes, the kids came into the kitchen. All that time, Nick had been making up with Abby. From her hidden smile, it seemed she enjoyed watching him grovel.

Stifling her own smile, Sarah brought

hot rolls and a salad to the table. She felt the tension build up once again as she watched the Logans dig in.

After his first bite, Brad asked if she'd made the casserole.

"Yes, of course. Is there something wrong with it?"

He shook his head and took another forkful. "Not a thing. It's great."

Sarah exhaled a tight breath.

The meal was perfect, just like she wanted, right down to the cobbler. The company was perfect, too. The Logans talked and shared their day's experiences, and the meal passed in easy conversation.

She didn't miss her stepfather yelling at her and the kids, and threatening them. She didn't miss it one bit.

Brad kept thinking about how well Sarah had fit into their household. From what she'd said, he hadn't expected her to understand how things were done here at the ranch.

After watching a TV program, he'd come back in the kitchen to find it spotless.

He even found cookies in the cookie jar. Waiting until his brother wandered into the kitchen, he sat down with a cup of coffee at the table.

Nick looked at Brad. "What are you eating, Brad?"

"Cookies." He held up an oatmeal raisin. "Sarah's doing a great job, isn't she?"

"I won't know until I taste the cookies," Nick said.

He joined Brad at the table with a mug of coffee and bit into one of the cookies. "Yeah, I think she's doing a good job."

Before Brad could answer, Sarah appeared at the doorway. "Oh, I didn't know you were hungry again."

"We shouldn't be," Nick said. "Dinner was great."

"Thank you, but if you need me to do something else, don't hesitate to tell me."

"Just keep the cookie jar full!" Brad said with a grin.

"I will. Um, Abby wants some cookies and some milk."

"I should've told you that she likes a late night snack. That's my fault."

Sarah fixed a tray, then carried them out to Abby.

"Is Abby doing all right?" Brad asked.

"Yeah, if I can just keep her down until it's time."

"Aren't twins supposed to come early?"

"Yeah, but the longer they go in the womb, the healthier they are."

"And one is a boy and one is a girl?"

"Yeah, fraternal twins."

"Is Robbie excited?"

"No, he's more excited about Davy. Of course he can see Davy. Right now, he doesn't really understand why his Mommy doesn't spend time with him."

"That's understandable."

"I guess, and he thinks when his mommy has the babies, he'll get to play with them."

"Well, after a while. Sarah said she's going to be here for three months. That will give Abby time to recuperate."

"I hope so. Mom said it takes a bit longer. And I want Abby completely recovered before she does anything."

"You may need to hire Sarah for a little longer."

"We'll see how things turn out."

Nick held out another cookie to his brother.

On Monday morning, breakfast was served by Sarah with no complications. Nick enjoyed not having to cook it himself. He expressed his appreciation.

Sarah thanked him, but she seemed too worried to appreciate his words.

"Is anything wrong, Sarah?" Brad asked.

She stared at Brad. "Nothing except that I'm leaving my siblings here with people I've only known for maybe five days, and they're starting school. And I'm going to face the man who choked my mother to death. Other than those things, everything is fine."

About that time, Kate and Mike entered the kitchen. Kate hurried over to Sarah to reassure her that everything was okay.

Brad didn't say anything else. He excused himself to go change into a nice shirt so he wouldn't stick out like a sore thumb in Denver. When he came back into the kitchen, Sarah stared at him.

"What's wrong?" Brad asked.

"I thought—I mean, you look nice."

"Thanks. Are you ready to go?"

"No, I have to finish the dishes first."

"I'll do them while you get ready," Brad offered.

Before Sarah could decline, Kate stepped in and shooed her away from the sink. "I'll handle this, Sarah. You go get dressed."

When she finally left the kitchen, Kate turned to Brad. "Did you pack extra clothes, son? You know, this could take as many as four or five days."

Brad shrugged his shoulders. "I guess I'd better pack more. You'd better tell Sarah that, too."

Kate had just finished the dishes and she volunteered to talk to Sarah.

Brad grabbed a leather jacket in case it got cold. Then he added a couple of dress shirts and ties along with a sports jacket. At that point, he figured he was done. He took his suit bag and hung it in his truck.

When he came back to the kitchen, he saw Sarah standing in the kitchen, telling

Anna what a nice time she would have at school and that Kate would take her to her new class.

"She's going to do fine, Sarah. Don't you worry." Kate put her arm around the child. "I'll stay with you as long as you want me to, Anna."

Sarah gave the woman a hug. "Thank you, Kate."

Brad tapped her on the shoulder. "Are you ready to go?"

When she whirled around, he could see the tears swimming in her eyes. "Yes, I can go now."

"Good. You want something to drink?"

She was trying to wipe away her tears. "Yes, that will be fine."

He grabbed a couple of cold drinks without asking her choice. He didn't think she'd make a choice right now.

"Where are your things?"

"In—in my room."

He found the small suitcase and brought it out to the door. But Sarah still hadn't moved.

"Ready?" he asked again.

With another look at the children, she finally moved out to his truck.

They drove in silence for half an hour, Brad not sure if she wanted to talk about what she was about to do in Denver. He figured it was best to get it out in the open and then move on. The silence was killing him. "Are you worried about talking to the police?"

She ducked her head and said, "No," in a soft voice.

"Okay."

Finally she said, "Will they give me guardianship of the children?"

"Mike said they're planning to. You need to ask that up-front. Sometimes police don't do as they promise."

"That's—that's not right!"

"I know it's not. But Mike thought I should tell you that. Maybe they'll be fair and treat you right. Just be sure you get their promises in writing."

She squared her jaw. "Believe me, I will!"

A few minutes later, Brad realized Sarah had gone to sleep. He figured that was a good thing. She probably hadn't been sleeping well. She seemed to be vacuuming and washing everything within reach.

Maybe after she faced her stepfather and received temporary custody of her siblings, she'd relax a little bit. It was a heavy load to be responsible for two kids before she'd even married. It would take a man with broad shoulders to take on that load.

He looked again at her. She was certainly beautiful, curled up in his truck seat. Soft, feminine, loving. With two children.

Focusing his gaze back on the road, he kept on driving.

When he pulled up to the motel the police had recommended to them, Brad reached over and gently shook Sarah's shoulder.

"We're here. I'm going to go in and get us a couple of rooms, but I didn't want to leave you sleeping."

"I don't need to go in with you?"

"No. I'll take care of it."

After he closed the door, she slumped back against the comfortable seat. She couldn't believe she'd slept all the way to

Denver. But she thought maybe she needed the sleep. She felt better now.

Tensing up when she saw Brad returning, she drew a deep breath.

"We've got two rooms on the second floor," he said as he got in the truck and started the engine.

When he parked his truck by an entrance with stairs, she opened her door and reached in the back seat for her suitcase.

"I'll get it," he told her, but she ignored him. With a frown, he got his hanging bag and came around the truck to meet her.

She asked him her room number.

"You have room two-fourteen."

"What's your room number?"

"Two-sixteen."

She didn't say anything as she went up the stairs. When she reached two-fourteen, she waited for him to open the door.

After he did so, he gave her her key. Then he left to go to his room, which was next door.

She'd just put her bag down and was looking around the serviceable room when she heard a knock. Suddenly realizing their rooms shared a connecting door, she opened it.

Brad lounged against the door frame with a cell phone in his hand. "I was going to call home and thought you'd want to talk to Abby."

Sarah nodded.

He punched in the numbers and waited for someone to answer. "Hello? Hi, Abby. How are things there?"

After a moment, he said, "Yeah, I'll let you tell her."

Then he handed the phone to Sarah.

"Abby? It's me, Sarah."

"I wanted to tell you what Kate told me about Anna. She was back here by ten because Anna was so comfortable. Her teacher made her feel good and helped her meet another student so she would have someone to eat with and ride home on the bus with."

"Oh, Abby, that's so wonderful! I was worried about Anna. She doesn't usually adapt so quickly."

"I knew you'd be worried, but your chicks are doing fine. Call back this evening and we'll put both of them on the phone."

"Are you sure? I don't want to be a bother."

"It will be good for the children, too. They'll want to know that you're in touch."

"Thank you, Abby. Are you staying down?"

"Of course. Kate came and fixed me breakfast and fixed a lunch and put it in the fridge. I just finished it. I think my hunger is growing!"

"If it is, it's because the babies need it."

"Thanks, Sarah. You know exactly what to say."

"Okay, take care of yourself."

She handed the phone back to Brad. After a moment, he hung up. But he still stood in the open doorway.

"We didn't stop for lunch," he reminded her. "Are you hungry?"

"I can wait."

"Nope. I'm not going to eat by myself. I'll give you five minutes. Then I'll knock again." He walked out and closed the door.

Sarah knew Brad was used to being in

control, but she wouldn't let him control her. Then again, he had driven her here.

This time when he knocked, she opened the door and smiled at him. "I'm ready."

They walked toward the restaurant next door, which the desk clerk recommended.

"By the way," he said as they crossed the lot, "Mike said for me to pay for everything. He thinks we'll be reimbursed by the police."

She stared at him. "Are you sure?"

"That's what Mike said."

"But just in case, I probably shouldn't spend too much. They might not pay for everything."

"Yes, you can, Sarah. Leave that for Mike to worry about."

"But he's trying to help me. I can't—"

"Want me to call and ask him?" Brad asked, pulling out his phone.

"No! No, I don't want you to call him."

"Then plan on eating a decent lunch. You need to be strong when you testify."

"Am I going to testify? I thought I'd just talk to the police and—and tell them what I know."

"I thought Mike had prepared you."

"Not to testify."

"What you'll do is talk to the police and then testify in a hearing to determine that your stepfather should be remanded to stand trial."

"And then I'll be finished?"

He shook his head. "If they hold him for trial, you'll have to come back and testify again."

Brad held open the door to the restaurant and Sarah went in. She stopped when a pretty young hostess stepped forward. "How many?" the woman asked her.

"Two."

Brad came in the door after her.

"Right this way," the woman said, smiling under her lashes at Brad.

After they were seated, Sarah said, "She was flirting with you."

"I know." Brad shot her a broad grin that lit up the gold in his dark eyes. "But don't worry. I'm all yours until we get back home."

CHAPTER FOUR

WHEN Sarah didn't respond to Brad's teasing, he decided he'd better keep an eye on her. He made sure she ordered a good meal. Other than that, there was no conversation during their meal.

She finished eating before Brad. He looked at the food remaining on her plate. "Don't you want any more?"

"No, thank you."

"You saving up for a big dinner tonight?"

"No."

"I was thinking…since we don't have anything scheduled this evening—"

Sarah interrupted him. "Of course you can ask her out."

"Ask who out?"

"The hostess. She's obviously interested."

"But I'm not. As I was going to say, I thought maybe we should go to a movie tonight. We don't have any theaters in Sydney Creek. What do you think?"

She stared at him, bewildered.

"Are there any movies you want to see?"

She shook her head. "I don't know what's playing."

"Did you go to the movies a lot?"

"No. I never went to the movies. It would've cost too much for all three of us to go."

Frowning, Brad asked, "Didn't you ever do things on your own?"

"Not after I moved back home."

Brad looked around. "I'll go get a paper so we can see what's playing."

When he returned to their table, he spread out the paper to the movie section. "What kind of movie do you like?"

"A happy one," she whispered.

He found a romantic comedy that had good reviews. "How about this one? Do you think you'd like it?"

"I guess so, but...I don't expect you to entertain me, Brad. That's asking too much."

"Then how about we entertain each other with a movie?" He shot her another smile that seemed to comfort her. Then, he asked the waitress about the nearest theater, got directions and went to pay the bill. He could tell that made Sarah uncomfortable. She seemed to stiffen beside him.

Once they ironed out their plans, he suggested, "Let's go back to our rooms and rest this afternoon. We've got half an hour before we need to leave to make the five o'clock show."

Sarah agreed.

He couldn't figure out whether she was actually looking forward to a catnap, or if she just wanted to get away from him.

It had been three years since she'd been to a movie, Sarah had figured out as she'd lain on the bed in her room before Brad had come to get her. Now she felt excited to go.

With Brad.

She glanced over at him in the truck and

wished she could see his face, but the falling darkness cast him in shadow.

Facing her rising excitement, she reminded herself that Brad was taking her to the theater because it was his duty. Still, it was nice to go. She realized how much she'd missed a night out since moving back into her mother's house.

Sarah sat quietly, watching while Brad drove in the traffic that Denver dealt with now. When he pulled into the parking lot at the theater, she breathed a sigh of relief. "I was afraid we'd be late."

"No, we left in plenty of time. We can get our popcorn and drinks and still be seated before the show starts."

"Popcorn? Drinks? But aren't we going to dinner afterward?"

"Of course. But you have to have popcorn when you go to the movies. And something to drink."

Sarah stared at him, her eyes wide.

"Come on, honey, we don't want to be late," he urged as he got out of the car. She emerged, too, and he came around to grab her hand, pulling her after him.

When he released her hand to take out money for the tickets, she missed his touch, but told herself he was just trying to hurry her along.

He bought a large bag of popcorn and two medium Cokes. She grabbed the bag from him and followed him into the theater. True to his word, they hadn't started the previews yet. Just after they sat down, the lights dimmed.

Brad pulled down the armrest on the other side of Sarah and put her drink in the holder. He'd already pulled down his. "Now, do you want to hold the popcorn, or shall I?"

Before she could answer, he said, "You hold it. That way, you can eat it easily."

So there she sat, with a handsome cowboy, in a dark theater. She never would've thought to be there.

"Mmm, the popcorn is good," he whispered.

She reached out and took a few pieces for herself. It was warm, well-buttered. Suddenly she found herself having a good time, despite the circumstances.

When they sat down to eat at a nearby restaurant, Brad acted as if their behavior was normal. "Did you like the movie?"

"Yes, I did. It was funny."

"Yeah, I liked it, too. Good choice."

"Did you like the little person?"

"Yeah, he was hysterical. Especially when he was being chased by the lion."

"Do you think that was a trained lion?"

"I think so. Otherwise how would you get any camera people to film it?"

"I don't think I'd volunteer even if it was trained."

"What if Anna or Davy were in trouble?"

"Well, of course, I would. Anyone would try to save them!"

Brad chuckled. "That's what I figured."

"I'm not a daredevil, but I'd find a way to save either one of them."

"And I believe you would." Then he said, "Eat your dinner."

"The hamburgers are good here."

Brad agreed, then said, "I guess we could've gone out for a good steak."

She shook her head. "I like it here."

A few minutes later, Brad offered some dessert.

Sarah had relaxed after the movie, but she raised her eyebrows at his suggestion.

"No, I don't think so. Of course, if you want some, go ahead, but I think I'm full."

"They've got a chocolate brownie sundae. We could share it."

The waiter smiled. "A lot of people share one of those. I can bring two spoons."

"Great. Let's do that."

After the waiter left the table, Sarah leaned toward Brad. "I don't think I can eat any of it, Brad. I'm really full."

"You can eat just a little, can't you?" Before she could reply, he added, "Abby said to call home tonight. We should call now before the kids go to bed." He pulled out his cell phone and dialed the number at home. After he talked for a minute, he passed the phone to Sarah.

She was relieved when Anna told her she'd had a good day. Davy didn't have a lot to say, because he and Robbie were playing a video game. Abby assured her all was going well. She found herself smiling when she hung up the phone.

"Everything's all right, I take it," Brad said.

"Yes." After a minute she said, "I really want to thank you, Brad. You've been terrific to me. I know you may have preferred the hostess sharing your evening, but I appreciate your sacrificing yourself."

"It's no sacrifice, Sarah, believe me. I've enjoyed myself tonight." Then he handed her a spoon as the dessert came. "Come on, take a bite. I can't eat all this by myself."

Distracted, Sarah did so. Her mind was on what he'd said. "I don't think— Oh, this is good," she said after a bite.

"Eat up. You're too skinny."

"Skinny? I don't think— Do you think so?"

He laughed. "Honey, you could put on twenty pounds and still be beautiful."

"Twenty pounds? I couldn't do that."

"Okay, maybe ten pounds."

She ate another couple of bites, but then she put the spoon down.

"Take one more bite for Davy. You know he'd love this dessert."

"Yes, he would. I don't think he's much bothered about what's going on. Anna is a little more concerned."

"I know they miss their mom."

"I guess so. She'd—she'd changed a lot. When Ellis got her started drinking, she'd become a different person. Argumentative and aggressive at some times, negligent and apathetic at others."

"I know you're doing the right thing."

"I'm trying, thanks to you and your family." She meant that compliment. She owed a lot to the Logans for giving her a place to stay, and even more to Brad for finding her and taking her in.

And for tonight.

This had been one of the best nights in recent memory. Dinner and a movie with a charming, handsome man seemed so out of place, given her circumstances, but Brad had helped her forget her troubles, at least in his presence.

After they finished their dessert, he drove them back to their motel and walked her to her room. "Will you be able to sleep tonight?" he asked.

She said, "Yes," but truthfully she wondered if she could. Not when visions of one particular good-looking cowboy danced through her head.

Brad had a lot to think about. If that had been a regular date, he'd have collected a good-night kiss, at the least.

And he'd wanted that kiss.

But his brother and Mike had told him to take it easy with Sarah. She had a lot to deal with.

He'd enjoyed their evening. When Sarah relaxed, she was a joy. He smiled as he thought about the evening. It had been a pleasure to feed Sarah. She looked like a strong wind would blow her away.

Stretching out on his bed, he wondered if Sarah had already gotten to sleep. She'd been tired, but she'd have to face the police tomorrow. He intended to be beside her every step of the way, to lend her support.

That was why he was here.

* * *

Brad was up early the next morning, as usual.

He hesitated to knock on Sarah's door until seven-thirty. Watching television seemed like a waste of time, but he wanted her to get as much sleep as she could.

When he finally knocked on her door, it opened almost immediately.

"You ready for breakfast?"

"Yes, I'm hungry."

"Good girl! Let's go eat."

He led her to the restaurant where they'd eaten lunch yesterday.

They ate without conversation. Brad didn't want to interrupt her breakfast.

When they got in the car, he said, "You got an idea of what they're going to want?"

"All I can do is tell the truth. Hopefully it will be enough."

"Good answer."

When they got to the police station, Brad guided her inside and asked for Captain John Lazerick. When he received directions, he led Sarah there.

"Captain Lazerick? I'm Brad Logan,

deputy for Mike Dunleavy in Sydney Creek. This is Miss Sarah Brownly. She witnessed her stepfather choking her mother to death."

The man shook Brad's hand and then Sarah's. "We appreciate your coming, Miss Brownly. We want to put this man away permanently."

"So do I."

"Right, if you'll come this way." The man turned to Brad. "We should be finished in a couple of hours if you—"

"I'm coming with her."

The captain looked at Sarah, who nodded. "All right, then, if you want to."

"I want to."

"Okay. Right this way."

For two hours Sarah answered the captain's questions, recounting what she'd seen that night when she'd returned from the grocery store, filling him in on what her stepfather had been like to live with, how he'd routinely threatened her mother and the children.

When she was finished, the captain

asked Sarah to take a lie-detector test. Brad stepped forward. "Why?"

"We just want to be sure. She's very calm, almost too calm."

Brad stepped to Sarah's side. "Are you okay with this?"

"Yes, thank you, Brad. I—I appreciate you helping me."

"Just do what you said. Tell the truth and you'll be all right."

"I will," she assured him with a firm smile.

They put her in a room with a window and a tester. Brad joined the others watching her.

He was proud of her. This wasn't easy for her, but she'd done a great job. She passed the test and Brad was waiting for her when she emerged.

"Good job, honey," he said.

She buried her face in his chest as he hugged her. "Thank you, Brad."

The captain said, "You did a good job, Miss Brownly. But you'll need to testify in front of your stepfather at the trial. Will you be able to do that?"

"Yes, I will. He killed my mother and I want him to pay for it."

"We want the same thing. Go get some lunch. When you come back, the lawyers will want to talk to you."

Brad took her arm and led her out. "Come on, I've found a good barbecue place."

"I'm glad to get a break," she whispered as he drew her along.

"I know. I don't know how those guys can do this kind of work. It's too much for me." After they got in the car, Brad added, "I think I prefer cows to murderers."

"Me, too, and I don't even like cows!"

He leaned over and gave her a kiss on her cheek. "I'll introduce you to a few of them when we get back home. You'll love them!"

A gurgle of laughter from her eased Brad's worries.

"I'll take you up on that, even though I don't know where we'll be living when all this is over."

They talked quietly while they ate in a small, nondescript restaurant filled with diners.

"This barbecue is delicious. Even their

veggies are good," Sarah said as she wiped her hands with a napkin.

"Maybe, but the beef is the good part."

"You are such a cowboy!" she teased.

He laughed, glad to see her relaxing again. "I hope so. I've been one all my life."

"Tell me about your life."

"Not much to tell. My dad and mom raised all six of us on the Logan ranch, at least until he died. He started me riding with him when I was three. That was when Nick got his own pony. We were both raised to be ranchers. Some of the other kids have looked for a different life, but not me."

"What's so fascinating about cows?"

"Well, there's lots of interesting things. You not only have to take care of the cows, but you also have to know horses. There's breeding of the cows and the economics of selling at the right time. You also have to manage your land so you have good pastures for the cows. It doesn't hurt to be a weatherman, too. And you need a good cook, so you can get the work done."

"Ah! Finally my skills come into play."

"They're pretty important, you know. They say an army marches on its stomach. That's true about cowboys, too."

"It sounds like a tough job, though. Don't you get tired?"

"Somedays, when the weather is rough, I'm really glad to come home. But I like my job."

"I think that's important."

"What kind of job did you have?"

"It was nice, but not exciting. They had to let me go because of the economy. I was a P.R. assistant."

"For whom?"

"An insurance company." She laughed when he rolled his eyes. "I told you it wasn't exciting, but...I liked it."

"Let's see, as housekeeper, you get to handle the kids, cook, do laundry and clean house. Are you all right with those duties?"

"Yes, I was doing most of them anyway, in addition to my job."

"Didn't your mom help out?"

"She used to. But after she had Davy,

she started drinking with my stepdad. She didn't do much around the house then."

"That must've made it tough for you."

"That's why the housekeeping job is perfect. I know how to do all of those things."

"Yeah. But if it gets too much for you, you need to let us know."

"I'll be fine."

Brad chewed some more meat. "I think they might need you more than three months. Would that be all right?"

"Yes. I want the kids to stay in school as long as I can manage it."

"That would be good. I think Abby is going to need help for a bit longer. Recovery from having twins is hard, according to Mom."

"Did your mother have twins?"

"No, but she had six kids. I think that might be as hard as twins."

She laughed again. "Maybe harder." After a moment she continued. "Tell me about your family."

"Well, there's Julie—she's the only girl—in Cheyenne. Charlie is in college.

Matt and Jason live at home with Mom and Mike. They're still in school." He shook his head and grinned. "I can't believe Mom still has two teenagers to deal with. And a new husband."

"How long have she and Mike been married?"

"About a year. Mom moved out and she and Mike built a place on the ranch land so they could be close. She wanted to give Nick and Abby their privacy, and let us get on with the ranch. She took the younger boys with her. And," he said, cracking a smile, "I suspect she wanted her own privacy."

"Kate is amazing. And so willing to pitch in."

"Yeah, she's pretty good. When Abby came back with Robbie, it was Mom who insisted she stay at the house. Nick was engaged to a terrible woman. I don't know what he was thinking!"

"What was wrong with her?"

"For starters, she was rude and thought she was better than us. She was a home economics teacher but never cooked and refused to clean. The one time she did cook, she used every pot in the kitchen. And there still wasn't enough to eat."

"So who cleaned?"

Brad grinned. "Nick. He got real good at that!"

Sarah couldn't stifle a laugh at Nick's expense. "That must have been difficult."

"Yeah. But he broke off his engagement and married Abby. He got a good cook, a great mother and a wonderful wife."

"That's a nice story, Brad. Are—are you planning on marrying, too?"

"I think I'll skip the part about bringing home a crazy woman who's a terrible cook. But yeah, I want to marry and have kids. Especially if they're like Robbie."

He couldn't ignore the image that flitted through his mind. Him bringing a certain brown-haired, brown-eyed woman home to meet his mother.

Now where did that thought come from?

CHAPTER FIVE

AFTER her drilling by the prosecutors, Sarah was exhausted. When she stepped out of the room with the attorney, she had a crazy urge to run right to Brad's arms.

He was waiting for her, of course. He'd sat in the room at the back while she went over her testimony. Over and over again.

As if he read her thoughts, he came up behind her and put his arms around her. "Good job."

"I'm so ready to be out of here," she whispered.

"Right this way. I know what you mean."

She wasn't sure he did, but she followed him.

In the car he headed for a suburb named Golden. When he started up a mountain, she thought maybe he did know what she needed. He finally came to a halt on a bluff that overlooked the city.

"Why are we here?"

"I thought you might need to see Denver from a distance. Get some perspective on the city."

"It's a beautiful view."

"It's also Buffalo Bill's grave site."

"Really?"

"Yeah. Come on. I'll show you."

They got out of the car and walked to the grave site.

"There's also a museum if you want to look in it," Brad explained. "But the view is what I thought was most important."

"Oh, yes, it is. Can we just sit for a few minutes?"

"Sure." He led her to a park bench and sat down beside her.

"How did you know I needed this?" she asked after a few minutes.

"I thought they were crowding you a little, back there. It made me think of this place. We came here on vacation one summer. Dad didn't want to be gone long from the ranch, so this was perfect. It's so peaceful and serene."

"Yes, it is." In fact, Sarah could feel the tension of the day easing.

They sat silently for another few minutes.

"What shall we do tomorrow?" she finally asked.

"Well, I thought we might go take the tour at the government building where they print money."

"Really? Is it interesting?"

"I think so. I spend so much money, I want to be sure they're printing enough of it."

She burst out laughing. "Oh, yes, definitely!"

"Seeing that much money will take your mind off Thursday."

"You're probably right."

"Then we can go to lunch. After that, we might come back up here, or I'll find somewhere else to go."

She drew a deep breath. "That sounds lovely."

"Did they bother you, the prosecutors?"

"No, not really. But they wanted me to

repeat my testimony so many times. I got tired of all the repetitions."

"I think you surprised them, being so strong and—and fierce in your testimony."

"Yes. I believe this is what I owe my mother. I couldn't save her from him, but I can make sure he's punished."

"Were you pleased that they're going to have the custody hearing Thursday afternoon?"

"Yes. I want to be able to tell Anna and Davy that they'll remain with me. I think that will reassure them more than anything."

"I'm sure you're right. I can't imagine them thinking about going back to their father's control. It would even frighten me."

"Poor Anna would go crazy. Davy… well, not much bothers Davy right now. But I think it would later."

She only hoped she didn't have to find out. She sighed. "I guess we can go now, if you want."

"I'm not in a hurry. It's cooler up here, too."

"Yes, it is, and it's very refreshing. I think I like cold better than heat."

"Then Wyoming is the place for you, since we have so much cold."

"Doesn't it make your work difficult?"

He grinned. "Maybe a little."

"Do you have many blizzards?"

"Sometimes. Everything shuts down until it ends. Then we go on as usual."

"How do you deal with that?"

"I've learned how. But you…well, you'll have to work harder, because we'll be there for every meal."

She smiled. "I think that might be fun," she said softly.

"You're my kind of girl, Sarah," he said with a grin.

Was she really?

Brad insisted they go out for a steak dinner that night.

"Are you sure we're not going over our budget?" Sarah asked.

"We have a budget?" he joked.

She wasn't amused. "Brad, we have to be responsible. They may not pay for steak dinners."

"I think they will. You're going to make

their case for them, Sarah. Without you, your stepfather would've skated on this, and they didn't want that."

"Neither do I."

"I know. Do you want an appetizer?"

"No, I think the steak dinner will be quite enough."

He grinned at her. "I bet you have a budget for each month."

"If I don't, we end up with no money at the end of the month."

"But you don't need a budget for the next few months."

"Why not? What if I spend too much money and you can't afford me? That wouldn't be smart."

"Nick is going to love having you as our housekeeper."

"Doesn't Abby have a budget?"

"Not much of one. She doesn't like budgets. When she was a single mother, she hated having a budget. She kept to it, but she hated it."

With a sigh, Sarah agreed. "I understand how she feels, but I'm afraid they're necessary."

When the waiter brought their steaks, they ate silently for several minutes.

Then, with a frown, Sarah asked, "Do I really have a budget?"

"Yeah, but it's a generous one. Nick didn't want Abby to worry. And I don't want you to worry, either. Relax. You'll do fine."

Sarah turned a bright pink.

Brad acted as if he hadn't noticed her embarrassment. "You know, I was thinking today."

"Yes?"

"Does your stepfather know you're going to testify?"

"I would think the prosecutors will have sent my name to the defense team."

"I guess they'd have to do that. But if that's true, why hasn't he pleaded? I mean, how can he expect to win if you're testifying against him?"

"I don't know."

"You wouldn't think he'd get a sympathy vote."

"I certainly wouldn't give it to him."

Brad smiled at Sarah. "Maybe they've

seen a picture of you and thought you wouldn't be able to testify in front of him."

"Maybe they think I'm not coming back for the trial."

"Guess you'll prove them wrong, won't you?"

"Yes." After a moment, she said, "I have to do this for my mother," and then added, "And for Anna and Davy."

"I know."

When they finished eating, they walked out to the car and he held her hand. Strangely enough, she liked the feel of her tiny one in his larger grip. With a sigh, she said, "I feel like going back up the mountain."

"We can do that," he assured her.

"No, I didn't mean— We don't have to do that."

Bringing her hand to his lips, he kissed her palm and smiled. "I think I feel like mountain climbing, too."

"Brad, really, I was just teasing."

"Liar," he said, smiling at her.

She didn't respond. He opened the car door for her. Then he came around and got behind the wheel.

"I think we should just go to the motel so we can get a good night's sleep."

"You're going to sleep at eight o'clock?"

"Well, I—I have to get ready for bed."

"Nice try. But we don't have to go tomorrow until about nine-thirty. The tour doesn't start till ten."

"Oh."

They drove in silence for about ten minutes. "Really, Brad, we should just go back to the motel."

"You got a favorite television program you want to watch tonight?"

"No."

"Oh, I thought maybe you wanted to watch *Desperate Housewives.*"

"That doesn't come on tonight."

"Aha! That is one of your favorite shows!"

"No."

"Then how did you know it's not on tonight?"

"My mother used to watch it."

He seemed to retract physically. "I'm sorry."

"It's okay. Really. I can't pretend she

didn't exist. And I'd much rather remember the good things."

Brad said he understood.

It wasn't long before he took the exit for Golden.

"Brad, you're making me feel guilty."

"Why?"

"Because you're taking me up to the mountain."

"Yeah, but it's what I want, too."

She didn't complain again.

When he parked, he came around to open her door. As she got out, he took her hand and shut the door after her. Then he led her to the bench they'd occupied earlier.

When they were seated, she tried to withdraw her hand. But Brad held on to it. After a few minutes, he brought her hand to his lips again.

"What are you doing?" she whispered. Somehow, sitting in this place made one speak softly.

"Kissing your hand."

"Why?"

"Because I like to. Because I like the feel of your hand." He kissed it again.

"Because I think you're very sweet and thoughtful. And because I believe you're strong for your brother and sister and because I want to be strong for you."

He kissed her palm this time, then up to her wrist.

If a gentle, harmless kiss like this could make her heart race and her mouth dry, what would a real kiss from Brad Logan do to her?

Brad didn't know how much longer he could wait to kiss her. Really kiss her.

He'd been on his best behavior the whole trip, gentlemanly and respectful. He even made sure he had her back to the motel by ten o'clock. He would've liked to stay out later, but he wanted her to get enough rest.

But when he took her to her room, he couldn't hold off any longer. He bent down and tasted her lips.

It was a little longer than a peck, but not enough to worry her. He hoped.

He remembered when he'd first seen Sarah. He'd thought she was a careless mother, risking her children for no reason.

But as her true story had come out that night, he'd found himself more on her side.

By the time they'd left home on Monday morning, he knew he was attracted to her. But Mike and Nick had warned him against flirting with her.

So he hadn't flirted. He'd been honest. And supportive.

He hoped that was helping.

It was killing him.

It was eight-thirty when he knocked on her door the next morning. She opened it at once.

"Yes, I'm starved," she said before he spoke.

"Good morning. Are you hungry?"

"Smart-aleck," she said with a grin.

"Yes, ma'am. Right this way." He smiled to himself. Each morning she seemed a little more relaxed. This morning, she obviously thought he'd waited too late to go eat. Tomorrow, he figured she'd be knocking on his door.

They ordered bacon and eggs, and when

he finished, he sat there watching her eat. She looked up and raised her eyebrows. "Is something wrong?"

"Nope. I was just enjoying watching you eat."

"I eat the same way you do."

"Nope. You're a delicate eater."

"You're making me nervous."

"Sorry. I just like to look at you."

"Brad! You're not behaving yourself."

"Are you going to tell Nick?"

She blinked several times. "Why would I tell Nick?"

He shrugged. "I don't know."

Though she gave him a suspicious look, she finished her breakfast silently.

"Ready to go, or do you need to go back to the room?" he asked.

"I'm ready to go."

"Will we see you two tomorrow?" the waitress asked as she took Brad's money. "It's not often that we get honeymooners!"

Sarah turned bright pink.

"Yeah, we'll be in tomorrow, too." Brad took Sarah's hand and pulled her out after him.

"Why didn't you say something?"

"Because the lady didn't mean anything by it. She was just being friendly."

"But we don't have rings on."

"Don't worry about it, Sarah. They don't know anyone in Sydney Creek."

She didn't say anything.

He opened the car door for her. "Come on. We don't want to miss the tour."

She sat quietly as he drove. When he parked the car, they both got out and walked to the entrance for the tour.

When they came out two hours later, Brad joked about the amount of money they'd seen.

"It's amazing, isn't it? It's hard to believe how difficult it is to get money when you see so much of it in there."

Brad smiled at Sarah. "It's us who put so much value on the paper money. After all, it's just paper."

With a big sigh, Sarah nodded.

"Now what do you want to do?"

She grinned at him. "Want to guess?"

"The mountain?"

"Yes, it makes my problems seem small."

"One mountain coming up."

All the benefits the mountain afforded Sarah the night before were washed away in a flood of tension the next morning. Brad could see it on her face and in the set of her shoulders as they made their way to the courthouse.

Knowing she had to testify against her stepfather with him in the courtroom ate at his gut. Sarah had already been through enough; he hated to see her endure more. But with any luck, she'd only have to lay eyes on the animal two more times. At the custody hearing later that day and at the trial, where her testimony would put him away for life.

As they walked into the courtroom, he reached for her hand. "Just relax, Sarah. You'll do fine."

She took a deep breath and let it out as she pushed open the door and entered.

The hearing seemed to take forever, probably because he wasn't permitted entrance. Pacing outside the door made him feel like a caged animal. When he finally saw Sarah emerge, he ran toward her.

Her smile through the tears told him she'd been successful.

"They've charged him and we're going to trial."

That was all he needed to hear. "Let's get out of here."

He took her hand and led her out into the sunshine. He knew exactly where to take her to celebrate.

They were back in the courthouse at one o'clock. The custody hearing started promptly, presided over by a venerable old judge. Luckily Brad was allowed in.

When Sarah was asked to testify, she could barely speak. Her voice quavered and broke. At one point she finally looked up at Ellis Ashton, seated at the table with his attorney, and stopped. Brad could almost see her demeanor change, strengthen, and when she resumed her testimony, she spoke with courage and conviction. He was so proud of her.

Then Ellis took the stand. Brad knew

any judge worth his robes would see through the garbage he hurled at the court. Under no law could a man like him deserve Anna and Davy.

Apparently the judge felt the same way. He named Sarah the guardian of the two children and promised they would send the official papers to her in a few days.

When they exited the courtroom, Brad lifted Sarah up and whirled her around. When he brought her back to the ground, she hugged his neck.

"Brad, we did it!"

"You did it, sweetheart. You and your stepfather," Brad said to her.

"Yes, he was my best witness, wasn't he?"

"Definitely."

She hugged him again. "Let's get out of here. I want to get on the road."

"Not yet. There's something we've got to do first." He handed her his cell phone. "Call the kids."

He told her the number and she dialed, nearly bouncing on her feet with excitement until someone answered.

"Kate? It's Sarah. We're finished and we're coming home." Her lips broke into a wide smile then and she blurted, "I did it, Kate. The kids are mine!"

CHAPTER SIX

"YOU realize the kids will be yours for life?"

After traveling quietly for almost an hour, Brad suddenly realized that. He didn't stop himself from voicing his thought.

With their mother dead and their father hopefully in jail for the rest of his life, she was all they had.

"Of course I realize that. That's why I had to win. I have to take care of them. They'll always be my family." He glanced her way and found Sarah staring fiercely at him, as if making sure he realized that she had accepted her responsibility.

"I understand that, but that means you have to make enough to support them. That won't be easy."

She squared her jaw and stared straight ahead. "I know that."

"Are you going to stay in Sydney Creek?"

"If I can. But when Abby doesn't need me anymore, I'll have to go wherever I can get a job."

"It's a heavy load."

"Yes, but they are my family."

"Okay. I just wanted to be sure you'd thought it out."

"I knew what I was doing when I took them away. I couldn't leave them in the home with that monster."

He reached out for her hand and squeezed it in a comforting gesture. "They're lucky kids, Sarah. They've got you."

Sarah didn't respond.

After a couple of miles he spoke up again. "Cheyenne's coming up. How about we stop and eat there?"

"Only if we go to the drive-through. I really want to get back to Anna and Davy."

Brad smiled. "I figured as much. That's not a problem. I can eat while I'm driving."

They stopped at a barbecue place and were back on the road in a matter of minutes.

They drove in silence as they ate. He looked at Sarah occasionally, but she kept her gaze on her food or the passing scenery. Was she avoiding him?

"Sarah, did I upset you?"

Her head spun around until she was looking at him. "No, of course not."

Then she turned away again.

He wasn't sure what he'd done. Maybe he shouldn't have pushed her about the reality of having the kids. But she needed to be sure of her choice. Not that he thought she was wrong. If something happened to Abby and Nick, he wouldn't hesitate to take care of Robbie and the twins. But he'd have help. His mom and Mike were there. And the other kids, Charlie, Julie, Jason and Matt, would all help, too.

He wasn't alone.

Sarah, however, had no one.

The realization sobered him. Made him admire her all the more. She was ready to meet the challenges ahead, no matter how difficult life became for her.

He'd never met such an amazing woman as the one seated next to him.

Despite his desire to tell her, he knew it was probably best to let that topic rest for now. Instead he chose small talk. "Was your sandwich good?" he asked.

"Yes, it was."

"Would you tell me if it was bad?" he teased.

"Probably, but it was good."

"Really? You always like everything. Are you being honest?"

That seemed to put Sarah over the edge. She snapped at him, "Yes, I am, and I'm tired of your attitude! You've provided everything I needed this week. Of course I liked your choices. You never once considered yourself. Did you think I didn't realize that? And now you want to complain because I liked what you provided for me? You're being impossible!"

"I was supposed to make this week easier for you. I appreciate your enjoying how we managed. It wasn't difficult to please you. But I have to say that can be bothersome. You never complain."

"That's because you have no idea how horrible my life was until I ended up in the middle of your family. I'm sorry you don't appreciate what you have."

"Hey! I appreciate my family! I know they're wonderful!"

"Fine!"

Brad was about to speak but stopped himself. When had they started arguing? And why? He didn't want to fight with Sarah, especially now, when they should be celebrating.

He decided not to talk at all, letting a long silence fill the truck cab. After a while he turned on the radio, found a football game and settled in to listen to the game.

It was safer that way.

Sarah leaned against the seat cushion and closed her eyes. She was disappointed with Brad. Back in Denver he'd been wonderful to her. But now he had insisted on presenting her future to her. She knew it was grim. She knew she'd taken on a lot. But she had no choice. She couldn't have left the kids there in the house.

She'd done what she had to do. All

along, she knew it wouldn't be easy. She didn't need him telling her that. Or pointing out how alone she was. But the three of them would make it.

Alone.

Without someone like Brad in her life.

She'd almost believed he cared for her. But she knew better now. He'd only taken her to Denver because Mike had asked it of him.

Once more, she was alone and responsible. And it would always be that way.

The family was waiting for their arrival. Abby had allowed the three children to stay up until Brad and Sarah returned home.

"Are you excited, Anna?" Abby asked, smiling at the young girl.

"Yes, I've missed Sarah." Anna's voice was still soft, as always, but there was an underlying sense of excitement.

"I bet she missed you and Davy, too." Abby took the little girl's hand in hers.

Nick looked out the window over the sink. "I think they're here. Abby, stay seated. You don't need to be rushing out to greet them."

"Yes, Nick, I know." Abby turned Anna's hand loose. "But you can go meet her, honey. It's all right."

Both Robbie and Davy joined Anna in running to meet Sarah and Brad. Nick stood at the door, watching. "Sarah just hugged Anna and Davy, and Robbie, too," he said with a grin.

"That's so nice of her."

"Now she's ushering the kids into the house."

"Good. I'm anxious to hear all the details," Abby said. "I can do that sitting down, Nick," she said before he could protest.

"I know, sweetheart, but you go to bed as soon as they tell us about the trip."

The group burst into the kitchen and Sarah came at once to Abby to hug her and thank her for taking care of the kids.

"They were very good, Sarah. No problem at all."

"I'm glad. And I'm thrilled I got custody of them. We're legal now." She turned to the kids. "You're going to be my children now. Okay?"

"Okay," Anna said with a big grin.

"What happened to Daddy?" Davy asked.

"He was taken to jail, Davy." Sarah looked Davy square in the eye. "What he did was very bad. He has to pay the price of his actions, and he probably won't get out of jail for a very, very long time."

Anna moved closer to Sarah, hearing her sister's words. Davy looked at her and then said, "Okay."

"Can we call you Mommy?" Anna softly asked.

"Of course, sweetheart. I'm your mommy according to the law. So it's official."

"But your name is Sarah," Davy said.

Sarah smiled. "You can call me Sarah or Mommy, whichever you prefer."

Davy nodded in agreement.

"Okay, it's time for you guys to be in bed," Nick announced.

Sarah said, "I'll help them to bed and then come back. Are Mike and Kate coming over?"

"Yes, Nick's going to call them now."

After Sarah and the kids had left the room, Abby turned to Brad. "Kate made a cake for your homecoming. Can you get down plates and forks for the six of us?"

"Sure."

"How did you and Sarah manage?" Abby asked as he set the table.

"Fine." He didn't add any details.

Nick hung up the phone. "Mom and Mike will be right over. I'd better go help Sarah settle the boys."

Kate and her husband arrived before the pot of coffee Brad put on had finished. When they asked how the trip was, all he said was "Fine."

Sarah exclaimed when she saw Kate's cake as she and Nick came back into the kitchen.

"Kate, that was so nice of you," she said.

"It's the least I could do. You must have done a great job in Denver."

"Thank you. I'm so appreciative of all your support. You've taken us in and given me a job and a place to live, taken care of the kids during this week. I couldn't ask for more."

She hugged Kate and Mike. Then she sat down beside Abby as Brad and Nick poured the coffee and tea.

"Oh, this cake is delicious," Sarah said.

"Brad, how do you like it?" Kate asked.

"Fine."

Everyone exchanged looks.

Then Kate said, "So what did you two do to entertain yourselves when you weren't in court?"

Brad said nothing.

"Brad took me to a movie. And we took a tour of the mint, saw lots of money, and we went up to Buffalo Bill's grave on a bluff above Denver."

"We went up there when we took the kids on vacation once." Kate smiled at the memory.

"It was lovely."

Brad looked away from Sarah.

"Well, the cake was delicious, and I appreciate all you've given me. But now I think I should head up to bed. Good night, and thank you again."

She left the table and went to the bedroom she shared with Anna.

As soon as she left, Nick turned to his brother and blurted, "What the hell happened?"

Brad said nothing.

"Did you and Sarah have a fight?"

"Not exactly."

"What exactly does that mean?" Nick asked.

"I did what you said. I supported her and stayed with her for all of it. But coming home, I thought she should realize what she'd done. So I questioned her about taking the kids, and how difficult it would be."

"You think she didn't know that, Brad?" Abby asked. "And what made you think she had a choice? Sarah loves those kids. Of course she knew what she was doing!"

"Yeah. So she told me."

"I don't blame her for being upset. Of course she had to take the kids," Kate agreed.

Brad threw up his hands. "Okay! Okay! I've got it. But it's not going to be easy to get a job that will pay enough for them when she leaves here."

"There are a lot of places she can be the

housekeeper. And room and board for the kids isn't that bad." Nick looked at his brother. "Is this going to cause trouble between the two of you?"

"Not on my part."

"Good, because we don't want Sarah harassed. I don't know what I'd do without her right now," Abby added.

"I understand. Did you miss me during the day, Nick?"

"Of course. I'm glad you're back before we got any bad weather."

"I've been wondering about that," Brad said. "I mean, what if a snowstorm comes and the babies come at the same time? How are you going to get Abby to Pinedale?"

"I don't know yet. When she gets close to the time, I may take her to a motel in Pinedale and stay with her as much as I can."

Brad nodded to his brother. "Right. I can take care of things here."

"Thanks, brother. It's good to have you back."

Sarah was up early the next morning, preparing a special breakfast. She was putting on the finishing touches when Brad walked in.

"Morning," he mumbled as he went past her.

"Morning," she replied. She saw him pour himself a cup of coffee and couldn't help thinking of how he'd greeted her back in Denver. And how she looked forward to seeing him.

"Want me to wake the kids?" he asked.

"That would be nice if you have the time," she said, with her back turned. Even to herself she sounded formal and stilted.

He left the room.

Sarah opened the oven and took out perfectly baked cinnamon rolls. She put them on the table and then started scrambling eggs.

"Wowee! What is that delicious smell?" Nick exclaimed as he entered the kitchen. "Cinnamon rolls!" He smiled at Sarah. "It sure is nice to have you back."

Sarah returned his grin. "Thanks."

He came close to pick at one of the buns but Sarah shot him an exaggerated leer. He pulled his hand back.

"So, you'll watch out for Abby today?" he asked.

"Yes, of course."

"I left you my cell phone number if Abby has a problem. We need to head for Pinedale if there's any hint of a delivery. It's only about six weeks before she's due."

"All the way to Pinedale? I thought you had a doctor here in Sydney Creek."

"Not yet. We've been growing, but we're not big enough to draw our own doctor."

"Don't you worry, Nick. I'll keep a close eye on her."

Then, running in front of Brad, Anna and the boys came in, dressed for school, and Sarah busied herself with their breakfasts. "You have to eat at least a spoonful of eggs with your cinnamon rolls," she reminded them.

Davy made a face and Robbie laughed.

Nick spoke up. "She means you, too, Robbie."

"But she's not my mama!" Robbie protested.

"Sarah is helping us out and you'll do as she says, or I'll be talking to you out in the barn, so we won't upset your mama."

"Yes, sir, Daddy." Robbie's hangdog air didn't bring laughter to Davy. He reached out to share his friend's feelings.

Within minutes, Brad picked up his cup and plate and placed them in the sink.

Nick looked at his brother. "Are you in a hurry this morning?"

"We've got a lot to get done. And I heard on the news this morning that a storm is moving in."

"What kind of storm?" Sarah asked.

"A snowstorm. It's early, so it probably won't last long," Brad said.

"But I don't even have winter coats for the kids," Sarah said.

"Don't worry," Nick assured her. "Robbie probably has an extra one for Davy. And we can check if Julie left one that Anna can have." Robbie took Davy to his room, while Anna followed Brad to his sister's room.

Each of the kids came back with a jacket that fit. Nick told them they could keep the coats. "Say thank you to Nick," Sarah told them, and she looked on them proudly when they did.

At the sound of a vehicle outside, she called, "There's the bus. Have you got your books?" She held out their lunches as they passed, and wished them a good day.

Since the men followed the kids out the door, Sarah finished cleaning up the kitchen. She realized how glad she was to be back. Even if Brad wasn't speaking to her.

Later, she picked up after the kids and decided to start a load of laundry. She finally got to Brad's room to collect the linens. He'd sort of made his bed, but she stripped it and gathered the dirty clothes from his trip. His scent clung to the sheets and the shirts, and she couldn't help herself. She buried her face in the fabric and inhaled. They smelled of the outdoors, of his cologne, of Brad. Surprisingly she felt nostalgic for their time together in Denver.

Until now she hadn't realized how much she missed Brad since their ride home.

She worked for another hour before Abby came into the kitchen.

"Cinnamon buns!" she exclaimed. "And to think I almost stayed in bed longer."

Just then, Kate entered, too.

"The smell of cinnamon does something to me!" she said with an exaggerated spasm of glee.

"I've heard it's the way to a man's heart," Abby said, playing along. She cupped her palms around her cheeks and turned to Sarah. "Is that why you fixed them for breakfast this morning?"

CHAPTER SEVEN

"OF COURSE not!" Sarah caught on quickly. "I fixed them for the kids."

"But did Brad eat one?" Abby asked, smiling.

Sarah jumped up to clear the table, hoping that would change the subject.

"I think Brad is particularly susceptible to cinnamon," Abby added. "It's a Logan trait."

Kate laughed, too, but Sarah shushed them. "You mustn't tease about things like that in front of Brad," she told Abby.

"Why not?"

"He doesn't want anything to do with me."

Abby's smile disappeared. "Why do you say that?"

"He made it very clear to me that I would be managing alone to take care of Anna and Davy."

Kate frowned. "That doesn't sound like my son."

"I'm sorry, Kate, but he left me in no doubt."

"Then, maybe, she's right," Kate said with a shrug.

"Okay, I won't tease you anymore."

"In that case, I'll make a special dessert for you tonight," Sarah said to lighten the mood.

"Does that mean we're invited for dinner, too?" Kate asked.

"I'm happy to welcome you, but I guess that's up to Abby." The more people there were, the less likely she'd feel the strain of her and Brad not speaking to each other.

Abby welcomed them, too. "Of course, you are. It will give you some relief after having to cook for all of us. Bring the boys, too. It's been a while since I've seen them."

"And I haven't met them yet. I still can't believe you have two more babies at home."

"Some babies," Kate said through a laugh. "Jason and Matt are already over six feet tall. Wait till you see them."

In her mind's eye the only six-foot-tall man Sarah saw was Brad.

It wasn't long after lunch on Saturday when Sarah had sent Abby back up to bed for a nap and threatened the kids with naps if they woke her up. She settled them in the family room in front of the television.

She was cleaning up after lunch when someone started banging on the front door.

Startled, she hurried to the front of the house, intending to yank open the door before the banging got louder. But something made her look through the peephole.

She gasped when she recognized one of her stepfather's friends, checking his pistol to make sure it was loaded.

Panicking, she ran back to the kitchen and immediately dialed Mike's number. He told her to lock both doors and get the .22 that Nick kept loaded.

After she hung up the phone, she found

the .22. It felt cold and hard in her hand and she prayed she wouldn't actually have to use it.

Then she remembered Nick's cell number, which he'd given her in case of an emergency with Abby. She called it.

It was Brad who answered.

"One of Ellis's friends is at the door and he has a gun!"

"Sarah, get the .22."

"I've got it, Brad, but—but I'm scared."

"We're on our way, honey."

She hung up the phone. When she heard banging at the back door, she moved into the hallway, so he couldn't see her. Robbie opened the door to the television room.

"Who's knocking?" he asked.

"Go back in the TV room and don't come out until I come for you." She knew her voice was harsh, but she didn't have time to explain.

She was trembling as she hid behind the hall wall, hoping the man outside would give up and go away. But she didn't think that was going to happen. When she heard the glass breaking on the door, she knew he was going to force his way in.

Waiting until she heard him open the door, she stepped out, lifting the rifle to her shoulder. "Throw your gun down."

"You don't scare me, little girl."

As he lifted the gun toward her, she squeezed the trigger on the rifle. Much to her surprise, she hit him in the shoulder and he fell to the kitchen floor, his gun skidding across the floor.

Covering her face with her hands, she sobbed into them, appalled at what she'd done.

Suddenly she heard footsteps pounding hard on the back porch. Brad came charging through, followed by Nick. He ran over to her and wrapped his arms around her. "Are you all right?"

"I—I think I hurt him, Brad! I didn't know what else to do. He lifted the gun up like he was going to k-kill me."

"You did what you were supposed to do."

"But Mike will arrest me!" she said with a wail.

"No, he won't, honey."

Just then they heard the sirens of the sheriff's car. "Here's Mike now. He won't arrest you, I'm sure."

She sobbed against his shoulder, in spite of his reassurances.

Mike stepped into the kitchen. Nick was bent over trying to stop the bleeding on the man's shoulder while Brad held Sarah.

"She shot the guy when he broke in and lifted up a pistol to kill her. She's sure you're going to arrest her."

"Sarah, it's all right. Calm down so I can ask you some questions."

But she couldn't seem to pull herself together, despite Brad's help. He got her some tissues and helped her to a seat at the table.

Mike's first question was "Where's the gun?"

"What?"

"If he raised his gun to shoot you, what happened to the gun?"

She pointed to the floor by the cabinets where the gun had ended up.

Mike picked up the gun and checked to

see if it was loaded. It was. He shut the cylinder and put on the safety. "Okay, how did he get in?"

"He knocked out the glass and reached in to turn the lock."

"Where's Abby?" Nick asked.

"She's—she's taking her nap."

"And the kids?"

Sarah finally remembered them. "Oh! I told Robbie to stay in the family room until I came for them."

Mike held up his hand to Nick, who was about to run. "Stay seated. We don't want them in here until we get him to Pinedale." He nodded toward the gunman on the floor.

Mike went to the phone and called his office, asking for a car with two deputies to come.

"Can you get me an old towel that you don't need?"

"Yes, of course." Sarah stood and went to the laundry room where she kept some rags for cleaning. She'd just put a towel in that pile this morning.

Bringing the towel to Mike, she stood there, as if she didn't know what to do.

Brad came to her and told her to sit down. "I've put on a pot of coffee. I'll have a cup ready for you in a minute."

"How—how did you get here so fast?"

"We were just in the next pasture when you called."

"I called Nick's number, but you answered."

"Yeah, I borrowed his phone to make a call and then forgot to give it back to him."

"I was glad you got here so fast."

"Yeah, but you managed on your own."

"Are you sure Mike isn't going to arrest me?"

"I'm sure, honey. He wouldn't dare."

"But I shot him!"

"Did you have a choice?"

"No," she whispered.

"Mike," he called to the sheriff who was talking quietly to Nick. "Would you tell Sarah that you're not going to arrest her?"

"Sure. Sarah, you're not under arrest. You were defending yourself. That's justifiable."

Relieved, she nearly slumped against Brad.

A few minutes later, the two deputies

arrived. Mike helped them ease the
wounded gunman into the backseat, the
towel staunching the flow of blood. Mike
told them to get him to the hospital in
Pinedale and stay with him until they
could bring him back. Then he came back
in the kitchen to call the hospital in
Pinedale, telling them the deputies were
bringing in a patient with a gunshot
wound.

Just then, a frantic looking Kate rushed
into the kitchen. "What happened here?"

Sarah had gotten a mop to clean the
floor. "I—I shot someone."

"Mike?" Kate asked, knowing he'd give
her the full story.

He did.

Kate reached out and wrapped Sarah in
her arms. "Oh, honey, I'm so glad you're
all right."

"I—I shot him, Kate!"

"You didn't have a choice. Of course
you did. That was the thing to do."

Sarah again burst into tears, this time on
Kate's shoulder.

They were interrupted again when Abby

woke up and came out to the kitchen. Before she could panic, Nick told her what happened. "Let's go get the kids," she said to her husband.

They reentered the room with Robbie wrapped around his parents' legs.

Anna ran to Sarah, hugging her around the waist. "Are you all right, Mommy?"

"Yes, sweetheart, I'm fine. But I'm glad you stayed in the television room until now."

Davy came over to Mike. "Did he have a gun?"

"Yes, Davy, he did."

"Then how did Sarah get away?"

"She had a gun, too."

Davy's eyes grew round and he stared at Sarah.

"Did she shoot him?" Robbie asked, just as in awe as Davy.

"Yes, she did," Mike said firmly.

Anna immediately burst in tears. "No! Don't take her away!"

Mike came over to squat down to Anna's level. "I'm not taking her away, Anna. She shot at the man because he was going to shoot at her. She didn't do anything wrong."

Anna continued to sob into Sarah's waist.

Mike reached out to touch the child. "Anna, it's all right. I'm not going to take Sarah away."

"You—you promise?"

"I promise."

"It's all right, baby," Sarah crooned to her. "I'm not going to leave you."

"I love you, Sarah!" Anna said, forgetting to call her mommy.

"I love you, too."

Brad put his arm around Sarah as her tears started to flow once more.

Nick came over to her. "You did a good job, Sarah. I'm sorry I didn't say that at once."

"It's all right, Nick. I should've known that, too, but I was too upset to think straight."

Mike urged everyone to sit down and relax and drink the coffee Brad had poured. "I'm going to call the Denver police. I think charges will be added to your stepfather's case."

Sarah nodded. "Good. I don't ever want him to get out of prison."

"I think we can all drink to that," Brad said, raising his coffee cup. The others raised their cups, too.

"Well, now that everything has settled down, I'd best get back to the office. After all, I sent two deputies to Pinedale. I'd better go protect the town."

Mike stood up and Kate rose to kiss him goodbye.

"I'll see you in a couple of hours, honey."

"Where's Grandpa going?" Robbie asked.

"He's going back to work," Abby assured him.

"Daddy, are you going back to work?"

"No, but I have to go unsaddle my horse. You want to come with me? I'll let you ride him to the barn."

"Okay!" Robbie said, jumping down from his seat.

Davy looked longingly after him.

Brad looked down at the little boy. "Davy, you can ride my horse back to the barn."

"But I don't know how to ride a horse, Brad," he said sorrowfully.

"It's all right, Davy. I'll lead the horse. You just have to hold on. It's easy."

"Are you sure, Brad?" Sarah asked.

"I'm sure, Sarah. He'll be safe."

"All right. Thank you."

Sarah watched Davy leave tightly holding Brad's hand. She knew how forlornly Davy must have felt seeing Robbie go off with his father and knowing his own father wouldn't be there for him. But his father had never been there for him.

She was grateful that Brad was reaching out for the boy.

"You don't feel left out, do you, sweetie?" she asked Anna.

"No, I don't want to ride a horse."

"Good. We'll just stay away from those old horses."

"But I think both of you need to learn to ride," Kate said.

"No, I don't think so, Kate. Who knows where we'll live after we leave here? We may be back in a city then."

"I hope not. I hate to see kids grow up in a city."

"We have to go where I can find a job," Sarah reminded her.

Neither Abby nor Kate responded to that statement.

When the guys came back to the kitchen a few minutes later, they found Sarah trying to decide what to fix for dinner.

"Honey, we're going to take you to the café for dinner tonight," Brad said.

"Why?"

"Because it's been a hard day," Nick said.

"But I don't think—"

"We'll call Mom and invite them to come, too," Nick said. "We all deserve a trip to the café tonight."

"But will Abby feel like it?"

"Where is she?" Nick asked.

"She went back to lie down."

"I'll go ask her," Nick said.

After Davy and Robbie bragged about their riding ability, they ran to the television where they could play their video game for a while.

That left Brad and Sarah in the kitchen alone.

Sarah quickly spoke. "Thank you for letting Davy ride your horse. That was very thoughtful of you."

"He looked so sad, I couldn't leave him out."

"I appreciate it."

"Have your nerves settled yet?"

"Yes, it took a while, but they're fine now."

Brad looked around the room. "Where did Anna go?"

"She went to our room. I think she was worn-out by her reaction."

"Yeah, it took a while for me to settle down, too. It was a relief to find you standing when I came through the door and had to step over that man."

"I know. I'm sorry that I called you. I don't know what I was thinking. I—"

Brad held up a hand. "Stop apologizing, Sarah. I'm glad you called."

"You are?"

"Yeah, and I'm glad you knew how to shoot a gun." He grinned. "Though I'm a bit surprised."

"Me, too. I've never even fired a gun

before today. I guess I just got lucky." But she knew the real reason for the shot. She'd had no choice but to protect the kids and herself.

"We'll correct that right fast," Brad said. "Starting next week I'll give you lessons."

"That's not necessary, Brad. It's not like I'll have to use a gun ever again."

"You never know, Sarah."

She could feel her skin crawl. Was Brad trying to imply that someone else would come after her? That Ellis would send a steady flow of gunmen till one succeeded?

"There are bears here, you know," he added.

She remembered him saying the same thing to her the first night she met him out on the government land. Back then she thought he was trying to make her life more difficult. Now she knew that she couldn't have been any luckier than meeting Brad Logan.

"Well, I'd better go tell Anna to put on a dress for our trip to the café." She stood up and moved to the doorway.

"Wait, Sarah," he called out, stopping

her. He lowered his eyes, and after a moment he said, "I'm—I'm glad we're talking again."

Finally he looked at her and she smiled into his dark eyes. "Me, too."

CHAPTER EIGHT

GEORGE'S CAFÉ was the only eatery in town. Downtown, it boasted good home-style cooking and a casual atmosphere. All the locals gathered there for oversize portions and neighborly chatter. That night was no exception.

The place was crowded when the Logan family and Sarah and the kids arrived. Brad insisted he and Sarah sit on one side of a big red booth with all three kids on the other. That left the other four adults to share a booth behind them.

Sarah leaned over to Brad and whispered, "Can Abby get in the booth? Maybe we should wait for a table."

"No problem. Nick's letting her sit on the outside so she can manage."

Sarah turned her attention to the three kids. "Behave yourselves. If you do, maybe you can have ice cream for dessert." The boys especially paid attention, as throughout the ride over they'd been giggling and shoving each other in the seat. Anna, sitting on the outside, just gave her sister a smile, but she frowned at the boys.

"Sorry, Anna, that you have to sit with the boys," Brad said.

"It's okay," Anna said with a shy smile.

"Good girl. What are you going to order?"

Anna stared at him, her eyes wide.

Sarah hurriedly said, "They haven't been to a restaurant before."

"You're kidding?" Brad asked.

Anna interrupted. "I get to choose what I want to eat?"

"Absolutely, sweetheart. Whatever you want," Brad assured her.

"I—I don't know. There are so many things."

"True. Take a little time and decide."

Anna read the menu to the boys and Sarah couldn't help but feel so happy. She was giving her siblings a taste of a normal life. From the looks on their faces, they were thrilled, if not confused by the many choices. The more they changed their minds, the more Sarah smiled.

"And what are you going to have?" Brad asked her.

She shook her head. "I haven't even looked yet."

"I've noticed," he said, reflecting back her smile. "Why don't you let me make a suggestion?" At her nod, he offered, "The Green Enchilada Casserole. It's Abby's specialty."

"Abby's?"

"Yeah. Before she and Nick were married, she worked here as a waitress and helped George come up with some new recipes. It's her best yet."

Everyone ordered the dish, except Brad.

Sarah looked at him quizzically. "You tell me to get it, then you don't?"

"What can I say? I'm a slave to a good steak."

"Maybe you should sit at someone else's table, then," Sarah suggested.

"Nope, I'm staying here."

Anna suddenly giggled.

"What's so funny, sweetheart?" Brad asked.

"You two argue all the time, but you don't get angry."

Sarah ducked her head, saying nothing.

"Why would we get mad?" Brad asked.

Suddenly Anna looked sad. "I don't know, but Mommy and Daddy always got angry."

Sarah reached across the table to take Anna's hand.

"I can't get angry at Sarah. She's too sweet," Brad said, grinning at the child. "Kind of like you."

Even though he didn't smile at Sarah, she felt the impact of it all the way to her toes. Brad Logan was truly a nice man, sensitive and thoughtful. The real man she'd come to know was nothing like the bear of a man she'd first met.

Sarah was so wrapped up in her assessment of Brad that she didn't hear the conversation between him and Anna till the end.

"I want to be just like Mommy." Anna looked at Sarah, love in her gaze.

"Thank you, sweetheart," Sarah said softly.

She promised herself then that she'd never do anything to diminish the admiration in the little girl's eyes.

After they placed their orders, the boys began wrestling with each other and Brad had to reprimand them. "That's not proper behavior at the dinner table, boys. When you get outside, you can do that kind of thing."

Robbie immediately thought to challenge his uncle by calling to his father. "Daddy, Uncle Brad told me I couldn't wrestle at the table!"

"He's right, son, and if you don't obey him, I'll take you outside."

Robbie pouted and Davy got very still. Then he whispered to Robbie. "What did that mean?"

"It means I get a spanking," Robbie explained.

Davy looked frozen with fear. "Sarah—"

"It's okay, baby," she said, reaching out for his hand. She knew he was sensitive to what had happened in his home, despite his cavalier attitude. Though she'd never seen Ellis hit the children, she knew he'd often threatened.

He held her hand tightly.

"Nick is just trying to make sure that Robbie behaves properly so he can grow up happy and successful." Not like your father, Sarah said to herself.

"Okay, Sarah. I will behave."

"I know you will, sweetheart, and Anna, too."

The little girl beamed at Sarah.

"I'm very proud of both of you," she said as she smiled back at them, her eyes glistening with tears.

"I think I'm going to pay for the Green Enchilada Casserole," Abby moaned.

The adults had all gathered around the table back at the Logan ranch for coffee. Abby had been uncomfortable by the time they'd returned from dinner, and Sarah had offered to put the kids to bed.

"But you said it wasn't hot, Abby."

"I know, but the twins don't seem happy."

"Will you be able to sleep?"

"I hope so. If not, I'll keep Nick awake all night, too."

Nick groaned, but he quickly put on a smile. "We'll make it, honey."

Brad said, "I can work without you tomorrow."

"We'll see. She may sleep better than she expects." He hugged his wife. "You know what might help you sleep? A big piece of cake."

Abby groaned.

The rest of them finished up the cake left over from last night.

As Sarah cleaned up the dishes, she heard Davy calling out to her.

"I'll go to him." Brad didn't even wait for her to reply; he simply walked out of the kitchen.

Sarah loaded the dishwasher as the rest of the adults said good night. Brad hadn't returned from Davy's room, and because she assumed he'd gone on to bed himself, she shut the light in the kitchen. On the way to her room she stopped by Davy's to check on him.

And there she found Brad. Curled up in

a chair beside the boy's bed, a children's book open across his chest as he slept.

He'd never looked more handsome.

The weeks flew by. Abby was now three weeks away from her due date. The doctor had told her that the babies would be good and healthy now that she had carried them more than thirty-two weeks. Abby relaxed a little, and Sarah encouraged her to rest most of the time.

Today was a different story. A storm had dumped snow and ice on the area overnight and made the roads treacherous.

Abby got up and began worrying. "I was always afraid I'd go into labor when there was a snowstorm like today."

"Are you feeling bad? Do you want me to call Nick?"

"No. I'm just worrying. Just ignore me."

"How about a cup of hot chocolate?"

"That would be great, Sarah."

Sarah fixed a cup of hot chocolate for Abby. "Do you want it in here, or do you want to drink it in bed?"

"Oh, in here, definitely. I'm so tired of being in bed."

"It's not for much longer. You've done a great job protecting the babies."

"Thanks. It's going to cut down on your work when you don't have to wait on me."

"I've enjoyed it, Abby. It's so nice to be around a normal family. Good for the kids, too."

"I don't know about normal, but I know we're happy. Nick is a wonderful husband."

"I agree."

"Brad will be just as wonderful as Nick."

Sarah felt herself stiffen. "What do you mean?"

"Aren't you interested in Brad?"

She tried to keep her cheeks from flushing. "No! I mean—Brad said he's not interested."

"Then why is he always helping you do things?"

"Because he's a nice man, that's all."

"Do you believe that?"

"Yes." She averted her eyes and got up to find some chore to do. Anything so she wouldn't have to sit here and talk about her feelings for Brad.

Truth be told—which she would never tell Abby or anyone else, for that matter—she was afraid she was falling in love with the cowboy.

When Abby pressed her, she turned back. "Frankly, Abby, when you don't need me anymore, I'll be moving on, looking for another job."

"But I don't want you to go!"

"Oh, Abby, you are so sweet. But you can't continue to support us just because you don't want to say goodbye. Maybe I'll be able to find something in the neighborhood. Then we could see each other again."

"I hope so."

"Smile, Abby. It's not the end of the world."

Abby dredged up a smile. "I guess. Are you sure Brad—"

As much as it pained her to admit it, she said, "No, Abby. Brad isn't interested."

"Then why did he sit with you and the kids when we went to the café?"

"Because he wanted to make it nice for you and Nick. It was a natural division."

"Why did he go with you to Denver?"

"Because Mike asked him to." She lowered her eyes so Abby couldn't see the disappointment there. "You see, Abby, I'm right."

"But—"

"There are no buts." She turned and left the room. There was laundry to be folded, lunch to be fixed. After all, she was here to do a job.

Throughout lunch, Sarah thought Abby was acting a bit strange. She wondered if she was feeling all right, or if she'd gotten upset about their earlier conversation. She hoped she hadn't crossed the line with her remarks.

After eating only bites, Abby went back to lie down. She had a book she'd been reading, and she wanted to read some more. But less than an hour later, Abby staggered to the laundry room.

"Abby? Is everything all right?"

"No! My water broke. Call Nick at once!"

Sarah helped Abby to a seat in the kitchen and then called Nick's cell phone. "It's time!"

The men had been working in a nearby pasture and she knew it wouldn't be long. She went to get Abby's suitcase, packed weeks ago for her trip to Pinedale, and put it in the truck. Abby was crying when she got back in the kitchen.

"It's going to be all right, Abby. Nick's on his way."

"I'm…having labor pains. Very close together."

"You won't make it to the hospital?" Sarah sat for a minute, thinking. Then she started gathering things.

"Sarah, what are you doing?"

"Getting some things together. I'm going with you to Pinedale."

"Why?"

"Because while Nick is driving, I may be delivering your babies."

"Have you delivered babies before?"

"My little brother, Davy." She remembered the day he'd been born. Ellis had been out cold, drunk again, when she'd come home to find her mother in labor. Davy was delivered right into her hands before the paramedics got there. She was never so happy to get help as that day.

About as happy as Abby looked now. "Thank you! I've been so worried!"

The back door burst open. Nick ran to Abby. "Are you all right?"

"No, I'm in labor, Nick. Hard labor."

"What are we going to do?"

Sarah spoke up. "I'm going with you, in the back seat with Abby. If she starts delivery, I'll help her while you drive. Brad? Will you come with us? If we get stuck on the road, it could save us. And can you call your mom to wait for the kids to come home?"

"Do you really know what you're doing?"

"Yes."

Nick lifted Abby up in his arms. "Let's get going."

Brad reached out for Sarah's hand, holding her while he made the call for his mother. Then he and Sarah followed Nick out to his truck. "Mom's on her way."

In the truck, the two men rode silently up front, Brad turning to check on Abby occasionally.

After one particularly long, hard pain, Sarah could see tears sliding down Abby's cheeks. She reached around Abby and placed a couple of pillows behind her. "Lie down, Abby. You're going to be fine."

Brad looked at Sarah. "Is she in a lot of pain?"

She nodded. "She'll settle down once we're at the hospital."

"I'm going to be driving fast, Sarah," Nick said from behind the wheel. "Keep her safe."

"I will, Nick."

Sarah pulled out the book Abby had been reading. "What page did you stop on, Abby?"

"I don't remember. She—she had gone in the silent house, feeling something was wrong."

"Ah. Here it is." She started reading, giving Abby something to think about other than her babies coming.

They had gone almost a half hour when

suddenly Abby screamed, "Sarah, I think one of the babies is coming!"

"All right." Sarah lifted her skirt and checked Abby. "You're right. One of the babies is pushing its way out. Don't push just yet. We'll see if we can talk it into not coming yet."

"I'm hurrying, sweetheart," Nick called to his wife.

"I know, Nick. Abby knows, too. She's fine."

A couple of minutes later, she said, "Okay, Abby, I need you to push, on the count of three. One, two, three."

Abby pushed. Then she drew a deep breath, ready to push again.

"Again. One, two, three!"

The baby slipped out. Sarah caught the baby in a clean cloth diaper, cleaning its airways, and the baby gave a cry, which gave Sarah a sense of relief. She laid the baby on Abby's stomach, leaving the umbilical cord attached.

Checking Abby again, she thought they had a little bit of time before the next baby came. She checked her watch and noted it was six minutes after three. "Relax, Abby. I think the second baby is going to wait a while."

"What's happening back there?" Nick asked.

"Your daughter has been born. She appears to be happy and healthy."

"Abby?" Nick called.

"Yes?" Abby said weakly.

"I love you."

"Me, too," she whispered.

"She's a little tired right now, Nick," Sarah said softly. "Brad, make sure Nick keeps his eyes on the road."

"Okay. We're not far from the hospital."

"Have you called her doctor?" Sarah asked.

"Oh, damn, no. I'll call right now."

"Let me call, Nick. You concentrate on driving," Brad said.

Sarah heard him talking to the doctor.

Suddenly Abby grabbed her hand again.

"Are you feeling contractions?"

"Yes," Abby said, almost screaming.

"Okay, I can see the head. When I say three, push!"

On three Abby began pushing again. Twice they went through the count and Abby pushed. The second baby came on the third push. She caught the baby and wrapped it up after cleaning it up. Then she checked Abby again.

She was bleeding.

"How much farther?" Sarah asked, trying not to panic.

"We're here," Nick said as he pulled up to the emergency door.

He got out and ran for the door. The doctor had already called and they were ready with a stretcher and two isolettes for the newborns.

Sarah drew a deep breath. She got out of the way as two nurses took the babies. "She's bleeding. I couldn't stop it," she told the doctor who came to Abby.

"We'll check her out."

She didn't even know who spoke, but she was glad to turn Abby's care over to professionals.

Nick went with her into the hospital.

Brad got behind the wheel of the truck and parked it in the emergency parking lot. Sarah stood there, waiting for Brad. When he reached her, she wrapped her arms around him, worried about Abby.

"What's wrong, honey? You delivered the babies all right."

"No, she started bleeding and I couldn't stop it!"

"Did you tell them?"

"Yes, but—but I don't know if they got it stopped!"

"Come on. Let's go in. We'll see what they'll tell us."

The nurse on duty said they'd taken Abby into the delivery room.

"She was bleeding. Were they able to stop the bleeding?"

"I'm sure they have. There will be someone out to talk to you when they've stabilized her."

They were directed to the waiting room where Sarah paced the floor and Brad sprawled on the sofa waiting for some news. Sarah hoped she hadn't messed up, but she hadn't known how to stop the bleeding.

Fifteen minutes later, she was still pacing the floor when Brad stood. She whirled to see Nick coming out to talk to them. Brad stepped to her side, putting an arm around her.

Nick burst into the room.

"Nick! Nick, is Abby all right?" Sarah asked.

"Yes! They stopped the bleeding and they're giving her a transfusion in the recovery room. And the babies are fine. The nurses wanted to know if you checked the time of delivery."

"Yes," Sarah said, swallowing her tears. "The little girl was delivered at 3:06, and the little boy at 3:10."

"Let me go tell them." He turned away, then spun back. "I almost forgot. You both need to come with me and see the babies."

They trooped to the nursery door. Nick told them to wait there and they watched as he went in and wheeled two isolettes to the glass. The girl was wrapped in a pink blanket, and her tiny brother was swaddled in blue.

Sarah tried to wipe her tears away, but they kept coming back.

"Are you all right?" Brad whispered against her ear.

She nodded, but she couldn't speak. She kept staring at the two babies she'd delivered.

"They're so small," Brad said softly.

"No, I think they're close to five pounds. If they're over five pounds, they can go home with Abby…whenever she gets to go home."

Brad hugged her to him. "She's going to be all right." He pulled back and looked into her eyes, his own shimmering in the light. "And so are the babies—thanks to you."

His hands cupped her face, and his thumbs wiped away her tears. "You are amazing, Sarah."

She couldn't say anything. She didn't want to ruin the moment, to break the connection between them. Instead she stood there, feeling as though she could drown in the depths of his dark eyes.

Then he lowered his head to her and she knew he was going to kiss her.

She'd waited so long for this moment. She closed her eyes and——

"There you are!"

Sarah jerked back in time to see Kate and Mike and all five kids come running into the nursery area.

"Oh, look, there they are!" Kate exclaimed as she peered at her grandkids through the glass.

Brad stepped closer to his mother, bringing Sarah along with him since his arm was around her. "Sarah delivered the babies," he said proudly.

Kate turned to face Sarah. "You did? Oh, honey, thank you so much." She gave her a hearty hug. "How is Abby?"

"She was bleeding, but they're giving her a transfusion."

"Good job, Sarah," Mike said.

"I—I hope so," Sarah said, tears running down her cheeks again.

"It's all right, honey," Kate soothed. "You did your best."

"Yes, but it may not have been enough!" Nick came out into the hallway just then. Kate immediately congratulated him and then asked, "How's Abby?"

"They got the bleeding stopped. She's getting a transfusion in the recovery room right now."

"But she'll be all right?"

"That's what they tell me," Nick said with a beaming smile.

CHAPTER NINE

"WHICH one is Sarah?"

Sarah looked up from where she was sitting with Brad in the waiting room chairs. A middle-aged man in scrubs stood among the Logans.

"I'm Sarah," she said, standing up.

"I'm Dr. Cartwright," the man said, walking toward her with his hand outstretched. "I wanted to meet the woman who delivered the babies."

Sarah swallowed before she said, "I tried my best."

"And you did a fine job. More importantly, Abby said you remained calm. I appreciate that, and I know Abby does, too."

"Thank you."

The doctor turned to Nick. "As soon as we put her in a room, you can go visit her."

"Thank you again, Doctor," Nick said, shaking his hand.

"I didn't do much. Sarah is the real hero."

"Oh, no, I just did what I could."

Brad put his arm around her again. "She's modest, but she did a great job."

The nurse came to the door, letting the doctor know Abby was settled in her room.

Then Nick came back and said, "We can go see Abby now. But the nurse said only two of us at a time. Mom, do you want to go in with me?"

Brad frowned as his mother went out with his brother. "I think you should've gone first," he told Sarah.

"No, Abby will want her family first. I think I'll go down to the shop and buy her some flowers."

"I'll go with you."

Leaving the kids with Mike, they went down and each of them selected a nice bouquet. Brad insisted on paying for Sarah's arrangement, despite her protests.

"Consider it a gift for taking care of my sister-in-law." He handed her one bouquet and he took the other. "In fact, I never did thank you properly, did I?"

Before she could say he had, Brad leaned down and kissed her lightly.

"That'll have to do for now."

Nick and Kate were walking out of Abby's room by the time they made it back. "Sarah," Nick called. "Abby wants to see you."

"I'll take her in," Brad said.

"Okay. Then I'll take Robbie in to see his mom."

When Sarah walked in the room, Abby called to her at once.

"I'm so grateful to you, Sarah. You sounded so calm. It helped me not to panic."

"Well, I panicked when I saw how much you were bleeding," Sarah admitted.

"But you didn't let me know. I appreciate it so much."

She took her hand and squeezed it. "And the nurse said both babies were right at five pounds."

"That's great news. They should be able to go home with you."

"I know." She finally looked at the flowers they held. "They're beautiful. Thank you both."

Sarah smiled at her. "Robbie's waiting to see you, so we should probably go."

Abby held out her hands. "I want a hug first."

Sarah hugged her, and Brad kissed Abby's cheek and hugged her, too.

They turned to go, and Brad whispered to Sarah, "I want a hug, too."

"You just got a hug from Abby," she said, confused.

"No, I want a hug from you."

She looked at him in surprise. "Okay." She hugged him before they went back to the waiting room.

As Nick ushered Robbie in the room, Brad stopped him. "If it's okay, I'm going to take Sarah home, and the kids."

Nick nodded his agreement. "Mom and Mike can drop Robbie off later. And listen, I'd like to stay here tonight, if you can manage at the ranch."

"Sure I can. Ready, kids?"

"But I didn't get to see, Abby," Davy said.

Sarah ushered him out. "You'll see her when she comes home with the babies."

"She's going to bring them home?" Davy asked. "Why?"

Sarah laughed as she tousled his hair. It was just the levity she needed after the drama of the day.

Two days later, Abby and the babies came home, brought to the ranch by Nick in his truck.

Sarah had cleaned constantly after she'd come back home that first night. She wanted everything to be fresh for Abby. She'd even added a sprinkling of perfume to the fresh bed linens.

She dressed up the kids and told them to behave and not to touch the babies unless Abby said they could.

"But I thought they would play ball with me!" Robbie said.

"Not until they're older, Robbie."

"But—"

"Robbie, just remember the rule. Ask your mother about touching the babies.

They aren't tough like you and Davy. They have to grow first."

"Can they talk?" Davy asked.

"Not yet, Davy."

"When you were born, Davy, you couldn't talk for a long time," Anna said.

"That's right. They'll soon be able to talk, but not this year."

Robbie crossed his arms. "I don't think I want those babies. They can't do anything!"

Brad came in in time to hear Robbie's remark.

"Sorry, pal, but you can't give them away. Your mom and dad love them as much as they love you."

"But, Uncle Brad, Sarah said they can't play ball or talk or anything. And we have to ask Mommy's permission to touch them!"

"That sounds about right," Brad said with a smile.

"Then what's the point of having them?"

"Do you remember when you picked your dog out? Baby? She couldn't do much then, could she? But you loved her anyway. That's how it is with real babies.

You have to take care of them until they can take care of themselves."

"Okay, but I don't like it."

Sarah spoke up. "Just don't tell your mother yet. It would hurt her feelings, and you don't want to do that. And that goes for you, too, Davy. We only say good things about the babies. Nothing bad."

"Okay, Sarah," Davy said grudgingly.

"They're here!" Brad called. He went out to help Nick with the suitcase and everything they'd brought home with them.

As Sarah stood by the door, she felt the cold wind blowing and thought of the fragile newborns. But Abby would have wrapped up her babies, she told herself. Then she remembered Abby had left without her own coat as they rushed to the hospital. She ran back to Abby's closet and picked up her coat and hurried out to Brad.

"What are you doing out here?" Brad asked.

"Here's Abby's coat for her."

He looked at her. "And where's yours?"

"I'm fine." She hurried back inside.

Nick carried Abby in and Brad toted in the babies. After everyone oohed and aahed over the infants, Abby asked for a cup of coffee. "I've been dying for coffee for nine months," she moaned.

"Can you, though?" Sarah asked.

"Absolutely. The doctor recommended I not breast-feed the babies because I have to take antibiotics for two weeks. Besides, as he said, how can you feed two at one time?"

"In that case, then, I'll pour you a cup of coffee right away."

Brad and Nick were each holding a baby, but while Nick's boy was sleeping, Brad's girl was fussing.

"That's Sarah Beth," Abby said. "She always wants food before Michael George."

Sarah stared at Abby. "You named her—"

"After you, of course." Abby smiled at her. "I wanted my little girl to know who had helped her come into this world."

"Oh, Abby, that's so sweet."

"So do you have a bottle for this young lady?" Brad asked.

"Yes, they're in the diaper bag, already fixed. Would you get them, Sarah?"

"Of course." She dug in the diaper bag until she found two bottles. "Does it matter which bottle she gets?"

"No. Would you mind feeding her?" Abby asked.

"Could I? Thank you, Abby," Sarah said, beaming as she moved to take the tiny little baby wrapped in pink.

Brad gave her a peck of a kiss before he surrendered her to Sarah.

She sat down at the table and immediately the baby took the proffered bottle. "You've already taught her to suck the bottle, haven't you, Abby!"

"Yes, I have, and she learned quickly. We have a little more difficulty feeding Michael. Brad, would you do the honors for Michael?"

"Come here, big guy. We've got to teach you to eat, so you can keep up with your sister."

"Brad, you shouldn't teach him to compete when he's two days old," Sarah protested.

Brad began to whisper to the baby as he fed him.

Halfway through the bottle, Sarah put Sarah Beth on her shoulder and burped her.

"Do I have to do that, too?" Brad asked.

"Yes, when he's taken about half of it, you should burp him, too."

"He's not there yet."

Sarah chuckled. "Way to go, Sarah Beth."

"Hey, who's teaching whom to be competitive?" Brad asked.

"I was just trying to be supportive of Sarah Beth."

"Yeah, right. Listen, Michael, that lady was making fun of you because you aren't eating fast enough. You have to work harder."

"Don't give him ulcers so young, Brad," Sarah said with a laugh.

Nick laughed at the two of them. "I can't believe you're worrying about how much he'll eat. That boy is a Logan!"

When the babies were about two weeks old, Sarah realized she had a problem. According to what Abby had initially proposed, she had about two weeks left on her job.

Not only would she be heartbroken when she had to leave, but so would her brother and sister. Anna was so attached to the new babies, and Davy would be heartbroken if he had to leave Robbie.

In an attempt to wean her from the infants, Sarah had begun to involve Anna more in what she was doing in order to shift Anna's focus. She had the girl help her make dinner or make a dessert. They were skills that Anna would need eventually, she rationalized. Besides, she had a knack for cooking and seemed to enjoy it.

One evening, Sarah let her make the dessert while she looked on for safety's sake. The chocolate cake was an easy recipe, and Anna had fun and felt proud when she served her homemade creation after dinner.

Brad in particular raved about it. "It's almost as good as your sister's," he said with a wink to Anna.

Anna beamed.

Sarah knew the praise was good for Anna's self-image; indeed, the child seemed to be coming out of her shell in the last two weeks. But Anna certainly didn't need more attention from Brad. He'd already gone out of his way to make her feel special. Sarah was afraid her plan might backfire.

Probably the best thing would be to simply bite the bullet, she told herself.

She had no choice but to start her job search and let the kids get used to the idea.

Herself, too.

Several days later, when Kate came over to help feed the babies because Abby was napping, Sarah asked her if she'd heard of any jobs in the area.

"You're not thinking of leaving yet, are you?" Kate asked.

"My employment here is supposed to be over in a week. I think I need to find another job, hopefully in the area."

"But Abby can't take over now. And it takes two people to feed the babies."

"I know, Kate, but Abby hasn't said anything and I'm supposed to leave at the end of the month."

Kate stared at Sarah. "I'll ask around. If there's a job to be had, I'll hear about it."

"Thank you, Kate." Sarah bent her head over Sarah Beth and placed a featherlight kiss on her downy brow. "I think Sarah Beth is really growing."

"Yes, so is Michael, and he likes his bottle now as much as Sarah Beth."

"Now you sound like your sons," Sarah said with a grin.

"It's amazing how quickly we've gotten accustomed to these two, isn't it?"

"Yes, it is." But Sarah was thinking about when she'd have to leave them. Would she ever see Sarah Beth and Michael grow up?

"You do realize the kids will be out of school in a week?"

Sarah jerked her head up. "In a week? Why?"

"Christmas vacation. It kind of snuck up on me because of the babies being born."

It had snuck up on Sarah, too. "I hadn't thought—I'm not prepared for Christmas."

"Me, neither," Kate said. "Thank goodness I don't have to worry about playing Santa Claus. Both my boys are too old for that. But Robbie still believes in Santa Claus."

"Davy, too. Anna knows better, poor baby." She remembered the day two years ago when their mother had told her. Anna had come home from school with questions, after a friend told her Santa was nothing more than a myth. Rather than prolong the childlike innocence, her mother had blurted the truth. Anna was crushed.

But that was just like their mother when she'd been drinking.

Sarah shook her head, as if to dispel the image. Things were going to change for Anna, and Davy, thanks to her. In fact, they already had changed.

After the babies had been burped and put back to bed, Sarah began making gingerbread men for the kids' after-school snack. That was the perfect treat for a child as the holidays approached, and she wanted Anna and Davy, and Robbie, too, to enjoy every bit of their childhood.

"It's nice that you're such a good cook, Sarah."

She thanked Kate. "I learned from my mother, before the other kids were born. She—she changed a lot after she had Davy. She was pretty good with Anna, but she kind of gave up with Davy." Sarah blamed her stepfather for that. He'd simply worn the woman down with his boozing and bingeing.

Before the kids came in, Brad walked into the kitchen.

"What are you doing here?" his mother asked.

"We've got a heavy snowstorm coming in. Nick thought it best for us to come in. I came to see if Sarah had a quick snack to take out to the barn."

"Yes, of course." Sarah began wrapping up two giant gingerbread men.

"I thought you made those for the kids," Kate said.

"I made some extras."

"Thanks, Sarah," Brad said. He turned to go.

"I think I'll walk with you, son." Kate

grabbed her coat off the rack by the kitchen door.

What was that all about? Sarah wondered. She watched Kate through the kitchen window and saw them stop to talk about halfway to the barn.

Then, suddenly, Brad spun on his heels and charged back into the house.

"Is something wrong?" Sarah asked as he swung open the door.

"Damn straight something is wrong!"

CHAPTER TEN

BRAD'S bellow seemed to shake the glass windowpanes as it echoed in the room, swept in by the strong wind. "What are you doing, thinking about leaving in a week?"

She wanted to shush him, to caution him about waking the babies and Abby. Instead she hurried to shut the door. She turned back to him slowly. For weeks she'd been thinking of ways to avoid having this discussion with Brad. Now, however, the time had come.

She looked squarely at him and said in a calm voice, "That's when Abby said the job would end."

He laid down the gingerbread men and grabbed her by the shoulder. "You can't leave!"

"Yes, I can."

"Where are you going?"

"I don't know."

"Then why do you want to leave?"

She gave him a furious look and shook off his gloved hand. "I don't want to leave, but this is how long the job is supposed to last. I have to find another job to continue providing for my family. I can't expect Nick and Abby to pay me when they don't need me."

"Damn it, Sarah, Abby can't even feed the babies by herself! How is she going to manage without you? And that doesn't include doing the laundry or cooking!"

"Brad, I'm not suggesting I have nothing to do, but that doesn't mean they'll want me to remain."

"I'll talk to Nick!" Brad exclaimed. He scooped up the cookies and charged back out the door, just as angrily as he'd come in.

Sarah drew in a deep breath, not even appreciating the aroma of baking gingerbread. Sadness and disappointment were all she identified. If only Brad felt about her the way she felt about him… Then she truly would be able to stay forever.

That, however, was not to be.

She wiped away the lone tear that streaked down her cheek and went back to work, hoping it would keep her mind off the handsome cowboy.

After a while she looked out the window and saw the snow had arrived. In fact, it was already coming down at a furious pace. She checked the time, worrying about the kids coming home on the school bus.

The same thought was on Abby's mind as she entered the kitchen from her nap.

"The bus lets them out at the end of the driveway. Will they be able to make their way home?"

"Maybe I should go tell Nick to get them."

Abby paused, considering her answer. "It probably wouldn't hurt to ask Nick. Do you want me—"

"No, I'll go." She ran back to her bedroom for a long brown sweater that buttoned up the front. She shrugged it on as she came back in the kitchen.

"Sarah, you can't just wear a sweater. Where is your coat?"

"This is my coat, Abby. I'll be fine. I'm just going to the barn."

Without waiting for Abby to comment, Sarah opened the back door and raced out into the snowstorm. By the time she got to the barn, she was shivering.

"Sarah, what's wrong?" Nick asked at once.

"W-we wondered if you should m-meet the bus. It's a l-long walk in the snowstorm."

"He's going to. Where's your coat?" Brad wanted to know.

She turned around to head back to the house, but Brad caught her arm.

"You didn't answer my question."

"No, I didn't. Turn me loose. I want to get back to the house. Abby's on her own."

"She's awake?" Nick asked eagerly.

"Yes, and the babies are due another bottle at four."

"Okay, we'll meet the bus. Don't worry about the kids."

"Thanks, Nick," Sarah said, smiling at him.

She pulled her arm free and headed to the door.

"Be careful, Sarah. We haven't put the ropes up yet."

Sarah turned to look at Brad. "What are you talking about?"

"The ropes so we won't get lost in a blizzard. When it really gets bad, you can't see your hand in front of your face."

"Will you be able to find the kids?"

"The bus won't leave until we get there. They'll probably stay on the bus until we drive up." He wiped snow off her shoulders. "Don't you get lost on your way back."

She looked nervously toward the door. "I won't."

But Nick stopped her. "It's about time for the bus anyway. I'll drive my truck to the end of the driveway." He turned to his brother. "Why don't you take Sarah back to the house and wait for us there?"

"Good idea." Brad grabbed Sarah by the arm and told her to stay right next to him. "I'll share my coat with you."

"No, I—"

Brad ignored her protest and wrapped his coat around both of them.

"You don't take up much room, Sarah.

Hang on." He opened the door to the storm and pulled her along in the near whiteout.

She had to admit she didn't feel the storm's bite on the way back from the barn. In fact, she almost wished the house were farther away. The warmth of Brad's body against hers was a welcome feeling, and she treasured every move of his hips against her, every hot breath against her head. By the time she made it back to the house she thought she could have melted the snow with the heat of her body.

When they got in the kitchen, she immediately moved away, afraid Brad would realize how much she enjoyed his attention.

"Nick is going to meet the bus," she announced to Abby.

"Oh, good."

"Abby, have you seen Sarah wear a coat?" Brad asked.

Abby stared at her brother-in-law. "No," she said, drawing the word out. "I don't think I have."

He turned to Sarah. "You don't have a coat, do you?"

"No, I don't. But I don't go outside that much!"

"Sarah, the winters here are severe. You have to have a winter coat." Brad shrugged out of his coat and stared at her, his hands on his hips. "If you can't afford one, I'll buy it for you."

"You'll do no such thing! I can buy my own!"

"Fine! Abby, I need to talk to you."

Abby looked at Brad, surprise on her face. "What about?"

"No!" Sarah protested, knowing what Brad was going to ask.

"Yes! It has to be decided."

"What is it, Brad?" Abby asked.

"Sarah thinks you're going to let her go after next week."

Abby stared blankly at Brad. Then she quickly shifted to Sarah. "Sarah, you can't leave me! I couldn't manage everything on my own."

"It's not that I want to leave, but you said three months. The babies are already two weeks, and I was trying to provide for my family."

"I'm sorry. I should've said—I still need you, Sarah. I'll have to talk to Nick, of course, but I'm sure he'll let me keep you for longer."

"Abby, I'm not trying to force you into anything. I just thought— Well, I was trying to plan ahead."

"Of course you need to do that. But I'd hoped…I thought you could just stay here!"

Brad turned around and faced the door. It was suddenly pushed open and three small snowmen, or in one case snowlady, came into the kitchen, followed by Nick.

"Nick, may I speak to you?" Abby asked urgently.

"Sure, hon, what is it?"

"In the bedroom, please." Abby got up and left the room.

"What's wrong?" Nick asked.

No one answered. Nick followed his wife from the room.

Sarah turned on Brad the minute Nick left. "You shouldn't have asked that question. I don't want Abby to feel forced to keep me."

"All I did was call their attention to

you leaving! Abby needs you. How can you leave?"

"I don't want to leave! But I have to provide for my family. If you recall, Mr. Logan, you've already pointed out to me how difficult that will be."

Anna stared at Sarah, panic on her face. "No! No, we can't go! School is wonderful. Can't we stay here?"

How had she allowed herself to talk like that in front of her siblings? She bit her lip, and walked over to Anna. "Honey, I don't know. We'll talk about it later."

"I'm not leaving," Davey pronounced emphatically. "Robbie and me are friends!"

"Look, we'll stay as close as we can, but they may not be able to pay me a salary, and I have to make enough to take care of both of you."

Both of them started to protest, but Nick came back out of the bedroom. "Sarah, may I talk to you a moment?" he asked.

Brad stepped up next to Sarah. "I'll come with her."

She turned to stare at him, but he wouldn't be deterred. He took her arm and led her to Nick as he walked out of the kitchen.

"Yes, Nick?" She expected him to tell her she had to leave. She was bracing herself for it.

"Would you be willing to stay here for the next year?"

"Year?" she asked, stunned by his offer.

"Abby thinks she's going to need help for at least that time. We can afford it, and I think it's a good idea."

"I—I'd love to, if you're sure." She was so stunned, she couldn't even smile.

"I'm sure."

"Good job, Nick," Brad said, whipping Sarah around for a hug.

"Brad, I don't think—"

"Come on, Sarah, I'm just being friendly."

"Yeah, Sarah, he's just being 'friendly.'" Nick grinned at Brad.

"Mind your own business, brother," Brad warned.

"Maybe you should tell yourself that, Brad," Sarah said sharply.

He gave her a cool stare, stepping away from her. "Maybe so."

Sarah watched as he turned away. She wanted to call him back, assure him she didn't mean it, but she held her tongue. But she'd just agreed to stay for another year?

Nick walked into the kitchen, announcing her decision to the three children. Davy and Robbie jumped around, dancing about the kitchen.

Anna came running in the hallway looking for Sarah. "Is it true, Sarah?"

"What, sweetie? Is what true?"

"Are we going to stay here for a year?"

Unprepared, Sarah said yes, but she wondered if it would be possible to do that. How long could she tolerate Brad's teasing and "friendliness" when she wanted so much more from him?

The snow continued all night. When Sarah got up to fix breakfast, she wasn't sure anyone would be up for it. Abby had warned her that if it was still coming down in the morning, school would be closed. They would wait for the snow to stop and the roads to be plowed before it would begin.

She couldn't see any reason for the men

to be up early, either. She put on a pot of hot chocolate for the children and a pot of coffee for the men. But she didn't see much point in cooking breakfast.

With extra time, she made cinnamon buns and got a head start on that evening by making a cake for dessert. She also tiptoed into the children's rooms to collect their dirty clothes and started a load of laundry.

She'd just sat down with a cup of coffee when she heard footsteps coming down the hall. She looked at the door, wondering who was up.

Brad stopped when he saw her. "I'm a little late this morning, Sarah. I hope it hasn't caused you any problems."

"No, actually you're the first one up."

"You mean the snow hasn't stopped yet?" He went to look out the window.

"Not that I've noticed. I haven't gotten the kids up since they won't have school today."

"And Nick isn't up yet?"

"I haven't seen him."

"Oh." He took a step back. "I guess I should—uh, go back to bed."

"That's up to you. I have a pot of coffee ready and some cinnamon buns will be coming out of the oven any minute."

Brad hesitated, staring at Sarah.

She kept her gaze on her mug of coffee, waiting for his answer.

"Thanks. I'll join you…if you don't mind."

"Sure," Sarah said, getting up to pour him a mug of coffee.

There was an awkward silence as they sat across from each other at the table. Finally Brad broke it. "When did you get up?"

"At six," she said, taking a sip of coffee.

"So you made cinnamon buns?"

"Yes." The painful small talk came to a merciful end when the oven timer rang signaling the cake was done.

"That's not cinnamon rolls," Brad observed when she took out the pans.

"No, these are cake layers for dessert tonight."

She dumped the cake layers on wax paper to cool, then went to put the washed clothes into the dryer.

Brad realized she had been busy all morning and still was.

When another timer went off, he called to her.

"It's the top oven," she called back. "Could you take out the cinnamon rolls, please?"

He did so, taking a deep breath to inhale the scent of cinnamon.

"Thanks, Brad," Sarah said as she came back in the kitchen.

"No problem," he assured her. "I, uh, might take a cinnamon bun to go with my coffee, if you don't mind."

"No, of course not." She took a cinnamon bun off the cookie sheet and put it on a saucer for Brad.

"Thanks," he said, sniffing the scent of the pastry with anticipation.

Nick came in the kitchen. "Smells good in here."

After their morning greetings, Sarah asked if Abby was awake.

"No. She got up with the twins at four. After they went to sleep, she did, too."

At his request she served him and took a

cinnamon bun for herself, too. Then she sat down at the table to enjoy some breakfast.

"She's also made a cake and is doing laundry," Brad said, nodding at Sarah.

"Maybe you should go take a nap, too." Sarah smiled at Nick.

"No, the kids will be up soon."

As if on cue, they heard footsteps coming down the hall.

Davy and Robbie came in first with Anna lagging behind.

Sarah gave them each a cinnamon bun and a cup of hot chocolate. Then she scrambled some eggs and fried some bacon.

When she heard Abby call her, she hurried off to help with the twins.

"I think Sarah is earning her salary," Brad said.

"Yeah, I think so. And she put a cinnamon bun away for Abby when she wakes up," Nick said with a smile.

"I want another cinnamon bun," Robbie said.

"Nope, that's for your mother. Time to go get dressed, kids."

All three children stood and left the kitchen.

"Not bad, Nick," Brad said. "You've got command of these kids at least."

"Except now you and I are going to clean the table for Sarah."

"Maybe you should've volunteered to feed the babies. That might be more fun."

"I helped feed them at four."

"Ah, you're right. Feeding them now would be too hard, wouldn't it?" Brad teased.

"You know, you have to change their diapers before you can feed them," Nick pointed out. "So I'm cleaning up, either way."

"Thanks for sharing," Brad said, laughing.

They cleared the table and rinsed the dishes.

Just as they finished, they heard someone coming in the kitchen. They both turned to see Mike coming in the door covered in snow.

"Mike! Are you frozen?" Nick asked.

"Yeah, I think so. Do you have any coffee?"

Brad went to get him a cup. "Is something wrong?"

"No, but the storm is slowing down. I'm going in to town in a few minutes after the snowplow goes by. I thought I'd stop and make sure everything's okay over here. Kate wanted to come, but she thought she'd better take care of the boys."

Both Nick and Brad laughed.

Soon they were all sipping the hot coffee, sitting around the table.

"Have you heard anything from Denver?" Brad asked.

"Nope, but I did mean to tell you that I've hired a new deputy, so you won't need to go with Sarah next time."

"No! If she goes to Denver, it will be with me!"

There was a complete silence for a while. Then Mike said, "I thought you would be grateful."

"*I* thought you two weren't getting along," Nick said.

"We're doing okay."

"Then what's going on?" Nick asked.

"I don't know what you mean," Brad said, trying to be nonchalant.

Mike stared at Brad. "I thought you'd be glad to be free of the escort service."

"There's not much to do on the ranch in the winter," Brad assured Mike. "Like today, Nick wouldn't miss me at all."

Nick didn't say anything.

"The reason I offered for my deputy to take her is that I've hired a new woman."

"A woman?" Brad asked in surprise. "What do you mean, a new woman? I didn't know you had any women!"

"I didn't, but I do now."

"Is Mom okay with that?" Brad asked.

Mike grinned. "Yeah. She's more okay with it than some of the wives of the deputies."

"Why would they object?" Nick asked.

"Well, for one, you haven't seen her. And two, I won't be working with her in a deputy car for eight hours."

"I see." Nick grinned.

Brad was stone-faced when he said, "I don't think she needs to accompany Sarah to Denver. I started it, and I'd like to finish it with Sarah."

"Finish what?" Mike asked, a curious look on his face.

CHAPTER ELEVEN

Brad felt himself tense as both sets of eyes stared through him. He was never so grateful for the sound of the women coming down the hall. He motioned that he didn't want to continue their discussion in front of them.

As Sarah entered the kitchen she came to an abrupt halt when she saw Mike. "Is something wrong?"

"No, Sarah, not that I know of," Mike reassured her. "How are you?"

"I'm fine, thanks."

"I just came to see how everything is with the twins. Are they doing all right?"

Abby smiled. "Yes, they're growing so much. They're asleep but you can come see them."

"I'd love to."

Abby led the sheriff down the hall so he could peek at the twins. Sarah stayed behind to put in a new batch of buns.

"Want me to make another pot of coffee?" Brad asked.

"Yes, thank you." She didn't even look at him.

He refilled the cups and brought the pot back to the sink to start a new pot.

"Thank you," she said softly as he walked back to his seat.

"No problem," he said, giving his usual answer.

Mike and Abby entered the kitchen. "Those babies are true Logans, Nick. They're growing like weeds."

"They ought to be growing as often as they wake us up to be fed." Nick looked at his wife. "Right, honey?"

"They certainly love their bottles."

"They're doing fine, Abby," Sarah said as she brought over a plate of hot cinnamon rolls fresh out of the oven. Mike couldn't help but take one when she offered him a plate.

"Thanks, Sarah. By the way, I've hired a new deputy."

Abby looked up. "Is it anyone we know?"

"I don't think so. She's from Cheyenne."

"She?" Abby asked.

"Yes, she's my first female deputy."

"Good for you," Sarah said.

"I offered to send her with you when you have to go back to Denver, but Brad didn't think that would be a good idea."

"*I* think it's a lovely idea," Sarah said, darting her eyes to Brad.

"I think you need a man with you!" Brad protested.

"You think my stepfather would attack me?"

"He's already sent one man to kill you."

"Isn't your female deputy able to protect me?" Sarah asked Mike.

"Yeah. She was trained by the Cheyenne police. She's quite talented with a gun."

"Then I don't see a problem with her taking over for Brad."

Brad stared at her. Then, without saying a word, he got up and walked out of the kitchen.

Sarah stared at the door through which Brad had walked.

"I didn't mean— Did I upset him? He was wonderful during our trip last time."

"Maybe you need to tell him that." Mike gave Sarah a direct look.

"Did he go to the barn?" she asked.

Nick answered her. "Yeah, he's probably working on tack, making repairs."

"I guess I'd better go apologize."

She ran to her room and put on the big sweater that she used as a coat. Then she hurried out the door before anyone said anything.

Sarah could tell the wind wasn't blowing as hard as it had been. Wrapping her arms around her body, she headed straight to the main barn.

When she reached it, she ducked in and looked for Brad. Finding him standing near the stalls, she moved slightly near him before speaking. "Brad, I— Can we talk?"

He'd gone out without his hat, and the snow had dampened his hair, turning it a darker brown. He ran a hand through it but didn't turn around. He continued working the tack.

"Brad, I didn't mean to hurt your feelings."

"You didn't!" he clipped sharply. And then he did face her, only to say, "Look, why don't you go back inside? This is no weather—"

But Sarah wanted to be heard. She cut him off by stepping into the middle of the barn where he stood. "I'm sorry, Brad, but I think I did." When he didn't protest, she continued, "You were great to me on that trip. But you and I both know that was only because of Mike. You wouldn't have accompanied me if it weren't for him."

"Mike had nothing to do with my being nice to you. I wanted to make the trip easy for you, Sarah. I thought you were being very brave."

He admired her? After the lecture he'd

given her in Denver, she figured he thought she was crazy for taking on the responsibility of her family. In fact, his insistence that she recognize the grave step she'd taken had told her Brad had no intention of doing such a thing.

She appreciated his admiration, but she didn't quite know what to say. She turned her attention to the stalls. "Why are these horses in here instead of out in the snow?"

"These are expecting sometime soon, so we want to keep them in, in case we need to help them."

Sarah was walking along the stalls, not yet ready to go back inside and not sure what to talk about. Suddenly she stopped. "Brad, isn't it a bad sign if a horse is lying down?"

"What? Which one?" he demanded, moving quickly down the aisle to the stall by which she was standing. He opened the door and went to the horse. "Easy, Lady Jane. Take it easy," he crooned to the mare. To Sarah, he said, "She's in labor."

"Can I help?" Sarah asked softly.

"Yeah, come on in the stall and pet her head, talk to her."

She did as he said. Kneeling down in the straw, she touched the mare's neck and told her all about Abby's twins, about little babies being so sweet, and she promised that Brad would help her.

A few minutes later, she looked at Brad and realized he was giving Lady Jane some help in birthing. She couldn't help watching Brad as he witnessed a birth from the mare. He was as gentle as he'd been with her during their trip to Denver. Only this time he was presiding over the birth of a baby horse.

Her heart swelled, as it had done in Denver. He was a good man. That was why she'd tried not to let her feelings overwhelm her. She knew he didn't want to mislead her. But she had to be careful and not take advantage of him.

"Here's your son, Lady Jane," Brad said, urging the horse to his feet.

Sarah moved back from Lady Jane's head and turned to look at the wobbly-legged foal. "Oh, isn't he beautiful?"

"Yeah, he is, but Lady Jane owes you. If you hadn't seen her down, we might not be looking at her baby now."

"All I did was ask you a question. You did the rest."

"Maybe we should just agree that we make good partners."

"I'm willing to do that, as long as all I have to do is have a conversation and you do all the work," she said with a smile. "What are you going to name him?"

"I think you should have that honor."

Sarah's head snapped up. "Really? You'd let me name him?"

"Why not? You deserve to be rewarded."

"Oh, that's a tough decision…. I think he should be named…Duke. Unless you don't like that name?"

"I like it a lot. Goes with Lady Jane, doesn't it?"

"That's what I thought." She smiled at Brad.

"So…are we friends again?" Brad asked.

"Yes, I hope so. I promise I won't take advantage of you."

"What are you talking about?"

"I'm talking about—about getting carried away when we were in Denver last time. I know you were just being nice, and I thought we had—had become friends."

"We had. I just wanted you to know what you'd done. It's a big responsibility you've chosen."

"As I told you then, I had no choice."

"I don't think—"

"Did you have a choice about helping Lady Jane give birth?"

"Of course not. It's my job."

She just stared at him, hoping he'd see the parallel that she drew.

"Okay, okay. Maybe you didn't have a choice. I just wanted you to think about it."

"I have."

"Brother, we have a new colt," Brad announced as they returned to the house.

"We do?" Nick asked. "Which mare?"

"Lady Jane."

"Did she have trouble?" To Abby and Mike he explained, "It's her first."

"Sarah is the one who found her down and alerted me. She came in the stall and petted her head and talked to her, helping keep her calm."

"Good job, Sarah. I didn't know you knew anything about horses."

"I don't. But I did what Brad told me to do."

"That's why I let her name the new colt."

"So, what's the name?" Nick asked.

"I thought— I chose the name Duke."

Abby clapped her hands. "It's perfect, Sarah!"

"If you'd like to change it, I'll understand."

"Well, I wouldn't!" Brad protested.

"Easy, Brad, no one's going to change the name," Nick said, grinning. "By the way, how does the colt look?"

"He's good. He'll look better in a day or two when his legs are stronger."

"I think he's beautiful now!" Sarah said.

"Spoken like a true mother, honey," Brad said with a grin as he wrapped his arms around her.

The three men had gone out to look at Lady Jane's first colt. Sarah stayed inside to start preparing lunch, while Abby offered encouragement.

"I'm glad you and Brad are friends again," Abby said.

"Yes, it's nice."

"What happened to cause difficulties?"

"I don't know. We just misunderstood each other, I guess."

"Well, I'm glad you've made up. I was afraid you wouldn't stay if you didn't."

"The kids wanted to stay badly."

Abby was silent for a moment. "But you don't?"

"Oh, Abby, yes, I want to stay, but—but when Brad was so hostile, I wasn't sure what I should do."

"I'm happy you made the decision you did."

"I'm glad, too, but it's one day at a time."

As Sarah worked, Abby asked her, "Are you sure there's nothing I can do?"

Sarah picked up a bowl and brought it to Abby. "Can you break up the walnuts for the salad?"

"Sure. These will taste good in the salad."

"I hope so. Maybe it'll help get the kids to eat their vegetables."

"You may have a hard sell there," Abby

said with a grin. "We'd probably have a better chance telling them they don't get any cake if they don't eat the salad."

When the kitchen door opened, Kate arrived. When Mike had agreed to stay earlier, Abby had invited her mother-in-law, too.

"What can I do to help?" Kate said as soon as she hung up her coat.

Sarah looked back at the stove and said, "You can butter the rolls before I put them in the oven. That would be a big help."

"I'd love to."

Then Sarah turned to the door and called the kids to come help, too.

Abby looked puzzled. "What are they going to do?"

"They're going to set the table for all of us."

"Do you think they can?" Abby asked.

"Oh, yes, certainly with Anna's help. She's quite good at setting the table, but I don't think it should be limited to the girl."

"No, of course not," Kate agreed.

The kids came to the door of the kitchen. "What?" Robbie asked.

"I want the three of you to come set the table for lunch."

"We're playing a game," Robbie said and started back to the television room.

"Robbie, I wasn't asking for you to volunteer. I'm telling all three of you to come help me by setting the table."

Anna came willingly and even Davy knew what was being asked of him. Robbie, however, remained where he was. "I don't want to."

Abby was embarrassed by her son's behavior. "Robbie, you are to do what Sarah asked you to do. You need to help do chores around the house."

"No, I don't, Mommy. I'm your little boy, not Sarah's."

"Then let me make myself perfectly clear. Help set the table for lunch, Robbie!"

"I don't see why I have to help her. Isn't she the housekeeper?"

Abby started to rise, but Kate urged her to stay seated. About that time, the men came into the kitchen.

Abby verbally pounced on him. "Nick,

you need to talk to your son! He is refusing to help set the table as Sarah and I asked."

"Robbie, why aren't you minding your mommy?" Nick asked with a ferocious frown.

"Because Sarah's not my mommy. We pay her to do things for us. We don't do things for her!"

"Nick, take him out of here. And don't let him come to the table unless he helps, like Anna and Davy!"

Sarah went back to work with her head down. Had she overstepped her bounds by involving Robbie in the chore? As their legal guardian, she had the right to tailor Anna and Davy's conduct, but truthfully only Abby and Nick could tell their son what to do.

Anna counted the number of people for lunch, then directed Davy to count out nine knives, nine forks and nine spoons. Sarah helped her take down nine plates and carry them to the table.

Davy helped her set. Sarah reminded him to put the fork on the left of the plate, and the knife and spoon on the right side. "Knife closest to the plate."

Nick came back into the kitchen with an unhappy Robbie. "Robbie wants to say something to you, Sarah."

"I'm sorry," Robbie said, not sounding like he was sorry.

But Sarah didn't challenge his attitude. She said, "Thank you, Robbie. Would you count out nine napkins, fold them in half and put them beside the fork at each plate?"

"Yeah," he said without enthusiasm. When he ran out of napkins, he plopped down in a chair.

"Robbie, you need two more napkins," Abby pointed out to him.

"Anna can get them!" Robbie snapped at his mother.

"Robbie, go to your room," Nick ordered.

"But I'm hungry!"

"Then if I were you, I'd get those extra napkins before Anna does!"

Robbie marched over to the napkins on the shelf and shoved Anna out of the way. Then he strode back to the table and threw down two more napkins.

"Son, you need an attitude adjustment. Let's take another trip to your bedroom."

Sarah was putting the lunch on the table, and the casserole she'd made smelled heavenly.

She put the casserole on the table and then turned to see if Anna was all right.

Abby said, "Anna, I apologize for Robbie's manners. They will improve shortly, I assure you."

"That's all right, Abby," Anna said.

"You are a sweetheart, Anna."

Kate concurred, "I agree. I did a poor job raising my sons, too. Only when Abby couldn't help with the dishes anymore, did I think to ask my sons to help."

"Sarah says since we both eat, we should both share the chores," Anna said, sounding smarter than her years.

Brad said, "I agree with Sarah. And we felt better when we shared in the chores, too."

Nick brought his son back into the kitchen. "Okay, Robbie, this is your last chance. If you can't be polite and participate in the chores, you don't get to eat lunch."

Everyone grew quiet in the kitchen, staring at the little boy. He stepped up and said, "I'm sorry I wasn't nice, Anna, when I pushed you. And I'm sorry I didn't act nice when you asked me to help, Sarah."

"Thank you, Robbie. That was a very nice apology. Now would you kindly take drink orders, you and Davy?"

While they were doing that, Sarah carried several dishes and a salad to the table. Then she took out the hot rolls and put them in a basket lined with a cup towel. She put the rolls on the table and asked everyone to sit down.

Much to everyone's amusement, Robbie collapsed in his chair, exhausted. "Finally!"

CHAPTER TWELVE

BY THE time Sarah brought out the cake she'd made that morning, Robbie had forgotten all his complaints.

She began cutting pieces of cake and the boy willingly got up to deliver the plates to everyone at the table.

Brad took a bite of cake and chewed it silently. Then he looked at Sarah. "This is even better than my mom makes, Sarah."

"Brad! You shouldn't say such a thing in front of your mother!" Sarah protested.

"Yes, he should," Kate said calmly, "because he's right."

"Oh, Kate, that's so nice of you."

Brad threw up his hands. "Sure, take her word for it, but not mine!"

"I don't think you should insult your

mother's cooking. She's such a good cook."

"I know that. I grew up on that home-cooking." Joking, he patted his flat stomach and flexed his arms, and Sarah couldn't help but notice how big and strong he looked. It was all she could do to turn her attention back to what he was saying. "But on some things, you're better."

"Don't you worry about hurting her feelings?"

"No. She's a confident woman." He winked at his mother. "Right, Ma?"

Kate slapped his hand across the table. "I think you both should stop arguing. That's what I think."

"Okay, Mom," Brad said.

Sarah just lowered her gaze and continued to eat her cake.

When the cries from the babies alerted Abby of feeding time again, Kate offered to help her with the twins. Mike got up to go on into town to work, kissing his wife goodbye first. The kids, at Sarah's prompting, carried the plates to the sink. She calmly accepted their help. When they finished, she thanked all three of them.

Brad watched all that, as did Nick. He wanted to be sure his son was helping as he should. When Sarah released the kids to go play, Nick went outside.

Brad called to him, "I'll be out in a minute." Then he turned to Sarah. "You did a good job with Robbie today."

She looked at him, surprised. "Thank you, Brad."

He still didn't leave. In fact, he got up from the table and moved closer to her. He was so close that she could smell his freshly showered skin. So close that she could see the gold flecks that shimmered in his dark eyes. So close that she almost lost her breath.

She tried to step back, but her behind hit the counter. Looking up at him, with nowhere to go, she felt her heart begin to pound and her mouth go dry.

Why was he standing there?

"Wh-what did you— I mean, is there something else you wanted to say?"

"Yeah," he said with a grin that made

those gold flecks dance. "I wanted to tell you you're doing a good job." Then he finally did what she was hoping against hope that he'd do.

He kissed her.

After craving it for so long, Sarah wanted to revel in the feel of his lips against hers, his body pressing into hers. But she knew she couldn't. Contrary to her desire, she pulled back. "Brad, you shouldn't do that!"

"Why not?" he asked a bit breathlessly, she noted. "Someone needs to tell you what a great job you're doing."

She put her palms on his chest to push him away. But when her hands made contact with his hot, rock-hard chest, she had to struggle to stay the course. She pushed him slightly. "I—I appreciate it, but you shouldn't kiss me."

Brad didn't move. He merely grinned at her. A grin that threatened to upturn her heart and swamp her emotions.

Just when she didn't think she could resist him anymore, he stepped back.

"Okay. I'll see you tonight."

And just like that, he left the kitchen. Leaving her swaying like a tiny ship caught in a storm.

She had to sit down in a chair before she fell. She didn't know why the man was kissing her. He'd made himself clear, in her mind, that he wanted nothing romantic to do with her.

Why, then, did he keep kissing her?

And why did she want it so much?

The next day everyone's duties were back to normal. Sarah got up at her usual time and had breakfast ready when the kids and Brad and Nick got up. Half an hour later, the children had left for school, the men for work and the house was quiet again.

After a second cup of coffee, Sarah got up and began tidying the house, emptying the laundry basket kept in each room. After starting a load of clothes, she went back to the boys' bedroom and made their beds. Then she went to her and Anna's room to do the same. Last came Brad's room. She smiled when she saw his unmade bed. He'd given up making the bed because she always made it up better.

Stopping in midstride, she noticed how rumpled it looked, how the blankets had been torn off and how one corner of his bottom sheet was pulled off. Hadn't Brad slept well last night?

Served him right, she thought emphatically.

Neither had she. Not after that kiss last night.

She finished his bed quickly, doing a cursory job. Then she left his bedroom and shut the door after her, feeling as though someone was chasing her. Going in there each morning killed her, little by little, smelling his scent, touching his clothes. It was the worst part of her day…and the best.

After lunch with Abby, she helped feed the babies. They took turns, and today she had Michael. As she held him, she realized how heavy he'd gotten.

Maybe Nick was right, she thought. Like a true Logan male, Michael would grow up big and strong.

Just like Brad.

No, she warned herself, don't go there.

After the babies went down for a nap, Sarah made a special treat for after school. Anna's favorite—banana pudding. Anna deserved it; she'd been helping out so much lately.

When the kids came in from school, however, Anna wasn't with them. She called Davy back and asked about his sister.

He shrugged. "I don't know where she is. Brad took her somewhere."

"She came home on the bus with you?"

"Yeah. But when she came off, Brad was talking to her."

"Where did he take her?"

Again, the shrug. "I don't know. He wanted to know why she was crying."

Sarah stared at Davy in frustration. "She was crying? Why?"

"I don't know." Davy looked at her, obviously frustrated. "Can I go watch TV now?"

Sarah walked with him to the family room. There she found Robbie. "Robbie, do you know why Anna was crying?"

He sat up and said, "I didn't do nothing!"

"Robbie, I didn't mean for it to sound

like I thought you did anything wrong to Anna. I was just asking if maybe you had some idea why she was crying."

He seemed to relax. "Some older boy said something mean to her at school."

"Do you know who?"

"Yeah."

Holding back her own frustration with the two boys, she calmly asked, "Can you tell me his name?"

"I don't think I should."

Sarah stared at him, wondering if she should press the issue or get Nick and Abby involved. In the end, though, she figured she'd let him be and go ask Anna herself.

She left the room and went back to the kitchen, keeping her eye out for Brad and Anna to return.

It seemed hours by the time she finally heard Brad's truck in the driveway. She ran to the door, waiting anxiously.

When Anna came into the house, she had a smile on her face.

Sarah hugged the little girl extra hard. "Are you all right, sweetie?"

"Yes, Sarah, I'm fine. Brad helped me."

And just like that, Anna moved on through to the television room, leaving Sarah stunned and still confused.

Brad gave her an odd look when he walked into the house. "What's wrong?" he asked.

"What happened to Anna?"

He shrugged, and Sarah wondered if that was a universal male reaction. Then he said, "The boys must've said something."

"Of course they did, but not enough for me to figure out what happened. But they said she was crying!"

He smiled ruefully. "Don't make it sound like I surmised something. Her crying clued me in. I asked her what was wrong. She didn't tell me, but I wouldn't let her get out of the truck without telling me after the boys went in."

"Well, are you going to tell me?"

"Yeah. A boy at school said her daddy killed her mother and tried to kill her sister. Anna started crying."

"Oh, my poor baby!" She felt tears sting her own eyes at the thought of the pain and humiliation Anna must have suffered. She hated Ellis even more now than she did before.

"She's okay now, Sarah."

"What happened? Where did you go?"

"I know the boy. More importantly, I know his parents. We went to his home and I asked Anna to go in with me. His mom was there and we confronted him in front of his mother. She was furious with him and promised to talk to her husband about his behavior. And she made him apologize to Anna."

"Oh, Brad, thank you. I wouldn't know how to handle that as well as you did."

"Is that all I get? A thank you? I thought I'd at least get a kiss."

She stared at him, wondering if it was really what he wanted. Finally she leaned toward him to kiss him on his cheek. He quickly turned his lips to meet hers and deepened the kiss more than she expected.

"Mmm, just what I wanted," he said, grinning at her when he pulled back. Then he went out the kitchen door.

Sarah stared at him, watching his long stride to the barn.

He'd done so much for her, but she thought he didn't want any attachment to her. And then he went and did something like letting Davy ride his horse because he realized the boy was hurt by not having a daddy to give him a ride, or helped Anna deal with the shame of her father and make sure she was protected by him.

Brad Logan was one paradox.

And one good kisser.

When she'd recovered enough from his latest onslaught, and wiped her tears, Sarah put the kids' snack on a tray and took it to them in the family room.

Anna, she noticed, wasn't there. Sarah left the tray for the two boys and took Anna's treat to the bedroom, where she found the little girl reading a book.

"Anna, look what I made for you today. Banana pudding."

"My favorite!"

"I know, sweetie." After a moment, Sarah said, "I talked to Brad."

"Oh, Sarah, he was so sweet to me, and he talked me into going into the house and confronting that boy. His mom made him apologize and she said she was going to tell his daddy, too."

"That was nice of him, sweetie. Brad is…very thoughtful."

"Yes, he is. He said you had enough to worry about. He was glad to stand in as my father if I'd just tell him what was wrong. Wasn't that nice of him?"

"Yes, Anna, it was, but—but we mustn't rely on Brad too often."

"He said you'd say that," Anna assured her with a happy grin. "But he said some things are just handled better by a man, rather than a woman."

Sarah was at a loss for words. Finally she said, "He might be right in this case. But we need to stand up for ourselves."

"Okay, Sarah," Anna said, but Sarah didn't feel sure that she had convinced her sister.

When she returned to the kitchen, Abby came in right after her.

"Sarah? What's wrong?"

"Anna had a little problem at school, that's all."

"What happened?"

"Some boy was teasing her about her dad being in prison after killing her mother and then trying to have me killed. She was crying."

"Find out who it was and I'll have Nick—"

Sarah cut her off. "No need. Brad already took care of it."

"How thoughtful of Brad. There are just some things men do better than women."

Where had she heard that before? "Yes, I guess so."

Abby looked at Sarah thoughtfully, but she didn't say anything else.

The men had come in from the barn, hungry and looking forward to rest, and Sarah was just about ready to call the children in for dinner when they heard a car pull into the driveway.

Brad looked out the window. "It's Mike. Think he wants dinner, too?"

Nick chuckled. "I can't believe Mom isn't fixing dinner for him and the boys."

Sarah had a feeling the sheriff was there because of her. She didn't think she could handle any more problems today. She'd had enough to worry about with Anna.

Mike came into the house, holding his hat in one hand and the other up in front of him. "No, don't offer dinner to me. Kate's got it waiting at home. I just came to talk to Sarah. I had a phone call from the Denver PD."

Sarah looked up, her face tight with tension. "What about?"

"Your stepfather accepted a plea. They said they wouldn't ask for the death penalty if he'd plead guilty for the murder of your mother and for the attempted murder-for-hire of you. So he'll be kept in prison for life."

Sarah finally took a breath, long and deep, and sat down. After several additional ones, she felt able to say, "Thank you, Mike."

"You're welcome, Sarah. You've held up awfully well."

"I wouldn't have without everyone's help." She looked around at everyone in the room. "You all contributed to it, and I want to thank all of you."

"It was our pleasure, Sarah," Abby said.

"In fact, I don't think we've done that much."

"I think you did, Abby. You took a chance on me doing a decent job at housekeeping. That made an immense difference."

"So, now what?" Brad asked.

Sarah stared at him. "I don't know what you mean."

"You don't have to stay here anymore. Are you going to honor the contract you agreed to with Nick and Abby?"

"Of course I am. Even if I didn't love it here, I owe them everything."

"You don't love it here?"

"No! I mean, yes, of course I do!" She stared at Brad, not understanding his line of questioning.

He smiled at her, as if she'd given the right answers.

She smiled back uncertainly, hoping that was what he wanted.

"Well, I'm glad to hear you're staying," Nick said. "I want my wife to feel rested."

"Nick!" Abby protested.

"Well, it's true. Sarah gives you a chance to recover."

"I know, but lots of women don't have that option."

"Don't worry, Abby," Sarah interjected. "I'm glad to provide the rest you need. You've done so much for me."

Abby hugged her. "Oh, Sarah, you are so wonderful."

"No, I'm just doing my job."

"Yes, but you always make it sound like it's a pleasure rather than a job."

"That's because it is. You've taken my family in and made us feel like we're a part of your family."

"Come on. Let's get food on the table," Brad said.

"Oh! Oh, yes." Sarah immediately began putting dinner on the table, with Brad's help, just as he'd done before.

Soon they were all gathered around the table. When dinner was over, Sarah asked her brother and sister to wait until the others had left the table. Then she told them the news that Mike had brought them.

"Okay," Davy said, showing no concern.

"Anna, how do you feel?" Sarah probed.

The little girl who seemed so mature

beyond her years once again amazed her. "I'm sorry for Daddy, but he did bad things." She shook her head. "I don't want to think about him anymore."

"All right. I wanted both of you to know that we're safe from him now. And we're a family. We're going to be all right."

"Okay," Davy said again. "Now can I go watch TV? My favorite show is coming on."

Sarah smiled at his innocence. "All right. Anna, do you like that show, too?"

"Yes. If you don't mind…"

"Of course not, sweetheart. Go with your brother."

The kids ran to the family room, and Sarah began to clean the table. She was carrying a first load of dishes to the sink when Brad came into the kitchen again.

"Oh! I didn't hear you come in," Sarah said, struggling to put the load of dishes down.

He ran to her and grabbed some from the top. His hand accidentally swiped her breast as he took the plates. "I thought you could use some help," he said, "and I see that you do."

"No, that's all right. You've been working all day. You deserve some rest."

"Why do I deserve some rest but you don't? You've been working longer than me, and you still have some work to do."

"Yes, but I have some time off during the day. I'm fine. You go ahead and watch television."

Brad, however, was undeterred. "I think I'd rather stay in here with you."

"That's fine, but you don't need to help me."

"I think I do need to help you, honey."

She began to protest, but he put an end to her objection by kissing her.

She jerked her head back. "Brad, you must stop doing that!"

"Why?" he asked calmly, innocently.

"You can't go around kissing me just because I'm the hired help! That's not right."

He looked at her quizzically. "Why do you think I'm kissing you?"

"Be-because I'm the hired help," she repeated, hating the fact that she stammered in his presence.

"Wouldn't that be pretty bad of me?"

"Y-yes."

"So, why haven't you objected?"

"You've been very helpful. I didn't feel you were always taking advantage of me."

"Did you ever think that maybe I was attracted to you?"

"No." Her heart pounded harder and she thought he could see it slamming against her blouse.

"Why not?"

What was he asking her? Too uncomfortable, she turned away from him. "Because you made it clear you weren't," she said over her shoulder.

He took hold of her arms and turned her to face him. "When did I do that?" His voice was like velvet as it settled over her skin, smooth and soft.

"You don't remember?"

"No." He shook his head and his scent enveloped her.

Despite the sensuous nature of the man in front of her, Sarah had to face the truth.

She dropped her gaze. "You pointed out to me that I would be alone with my burden."

Brad's voice sharpened and turned taut. "And you thought that meant I wasn't interested in you?"

"Of course that's what you meant!" she returned.

"No, that's not what I meant. I just wanted you to know the reality of what you had taken on."

"That's what I said!"

"I didn't mean I didn't have feelings for you. I had promised Nick and Mike not to show any interest in you until you had the problem with your stepfather all settled."

"I don't understand," Sarah said, frowning. Her head felt as if it were swimming.

Brad let his hands slip down her arms and he gripped her hands in his. "Honey, I received strict instructions that I shouldn't flirt with you. I tried my best—" he smiled that devilish smile at her "—but sometimes you were just too cute. So, on the way home, I thought I should make sure you realized what you did. I didn't mean to make you angry."

"Make me angry? You broke my heart!"

She slugged him in the arm. "And you confused me every time you kissed me!"

"Does that mean you liked it?" Brad said as he rubbed his arm.

"No!" she shouted and turned her back on him.

"Not even a little?" he teased with a singsong voice.

"How could you do that to me, Brad Logan?"

"I wasn't trying to confuse you, honey, but how could I not kiss you when you did such wonderful things like deliver the twins? Or come out to apologize to me in the barn and end up helping deliver the colt?"

She sniffed, lowering her head from his eyes.

He crooked his index finger and put it under her chin, lifting her face to his once again. His eyes were dark and serious when he said, "I had to make sure you didn't start looking around for another man to help you. If I was going to hold back, I wanted to make sure no one else took advantage."

"That makes me sound terrible!"

"You don't realize how wonderful you are. You've done anything Nick and Abby asked *and* delivered their twins!"

"That was an accident."

"Yeah, but you came through."

Brad opened his mouth to continue, but Nick and Abby's entry into the kitchen interrupted him.

They were discussing something and didn't look up for a minute. But Sarah figured they heard her indrawn breath.

"Uh, hi, guys," Nick said, all smiles. "Is there a pot of decaf?"

"No, but—but I'll put one on," Sarah said hurriedly and she stepped away from Brad. She didn't want to see the look on his face.

They sat down at the table, and Abby started telling Sarah about how well the babies had taken their bottles.

Her mind wandered, though, and all she could think about was her conversation with Brad, and his kiss.

"Don't you think, Sarah?"

She looked up when she heard her name. "Sorry, Abby?"

Abby gave her a strange look. "Are you feeling all right, Sarah? You look a little flushed."

Her hands flew to her cheeks. "Y-yes, of course."

"She should tell you that you interrupted a private conversation!" Brad said emphatically, obviously not able to play along anymore.

"Oh! Do you want us to take our coffee to the family room?" Abby asked.

"Of course not," Sarah said.

Nick looked at his brother. "What do you think, Brad? Want us to go away?"

"He doesn't want that, I'm sure." Sarah glared at Brad.

He sighed. "I guess we'll join you for coffee."

Abby stared at Brad, obviously wanting to know what they had been discussing. But she didn't ask.

Brad told his brother and his wife what they wanted to know. "We were talking about our relationship."

"And how's it going?" Nick asked, sinking back in his chair with a grin.

"She thinks I don't care anything about her. And that's your fault, brother. Yours and Mike's."

"Whoa! We didn't— Well, maybe we did, but we thought if you put your hands on her, she might not be able to deal with it."

Abby swatted her husband. "Nick! How could you?"

"It doesn't matter," Sarah said flatly, trying to defuse the argument.

"Don't say that, sweetheart," Brad said.

"Why? It's the truth, which is more than you've been saying!"

"Sarah, I was trying to ease you into the fact that I want to marry you, but you keep fighting me!"

"I do not fight you. You hadn't mentioned marriage until now."

"I felt I had to wait until you either went to Denver for the trial or they told you it was settled. If I had to take you to Denver, I had to remain indifferent to you, and I hadn't done a good job on the indifference part so far."

"I think you were perfectly indifferent!"

Brad protested, but Sarah got up to pour the coffee. Instead of reaching the cabinet, she ended up in Brad's lap.

"What are you doing, Brad?" she demanded.

"I've decided to stop fooling around." And right there, in front of everyone, he swooped her back in his arms and kissed her.

Sarah knew she wasn't doing a good job of resisting. It wasn't something new. Every time he'd kissed her, she'd wanted to throw her arms around his neck. But this kiss was unlike all the others. This kiss felt very real. And she didn't want it to end.

When Brad finally pulled his lips away, he whispered in her ear, "Will you marry me?"

She could hardly believe she was hearing those words from his lips. Still, as happy as she was, she had Anna and Davy to think about. "I want to, Brad. Very much. But Anna and Davy will always be part of my family."

"Don't you know that I've taken them in to my family? I think we'll make a great family. And I think it's about time we get married. After all, we have a nine-year-old already!"

"Brad, you know that's not true," Sarah said, laughing.

Brad grinned at her. "Is Anna nine?"

'Yes, of course, but—"

"Then I guess we have a nine-year-old daughter."

"Brad, you are the sweetest man I know," Sarah said before she kissed him.

Abby whispered to her husband, "I think they're managing all right, even with an audience."

"Yeah, but I still haven't gotten my coffee."

Sarah jumped off Brad's lap to pour the coffee.

"Hey, tell my brother to go away and you come back to my lap, young lady!"

Sarah smiled at Brad. "I can't serve coffee and sit in your lap at the same time."

She poured and Brad carried the cups to the table. He tempted her into his lap once again with his outstretched arms, but she sidestepped him this time, taking her own chair, though it was right next to his.

"I suddenly feel like we're interrupting something," Nick said to his wife, acting dense.

"Does that mean you're going to leave?" Brad asked him.

"No, not after the hard time you gave me when I was courting Abby."

"You weren't courting Abby. You were courting Patricia, though I couldn't understand why. At least I've made the right choice."

"That's because I've been a better example for you."

Brad glared at his brother. "Have you finished your coffee yet?"

"Nope. I like to savor my coffee."

"Fine! Then Sarah and I will go to my bedroom so we can have some privacy!"

As he got up to grab Sarah, Abby shouted, "No! I can't let you take Sarah to your bedroom."

Brad looked at Sarah with pleading in his eyes. "Come on, Sarah. Tell Abby you'll be good."

"And what do you tell Anna if she sees me going to your bedroom?"

"Tell her I'm going to be her daddy. That's all she needs to know."

"So when she grows up and wants to go to a single man's bedroom, you'll say…"

Brad shook his head. "Damn it, we'd better get married in a hurry."

Sarah grinned at him. "I don't think I've said yes, just yet."

He leaned over and kissed her again. In no time, she was wrapped up in his arms. When he released her that time, after several minutes, he said, "I don't know how long I can kiss you in public and behave myself."

"And that's why you can't take her to your bedroom!" Abby announced.

"Maybe I'd better say yes."

"I'm all for it," he said and pulled her from her chair into his lap, wrapping his arms around her and kissing her deeply.

"And maybe we'd better finish our coffee, so these two lovebirds can enjoy themselves," Nick said finally. "Welcome to the family, Sarah."

"Thank you, Nick," Sarah said, smiling broadly. Those words sounded so good to her ears.

"Me, too, Sarah. This is what I was hoping for all along."

"Me, too, Abby. I finally found a friend who'll last my lifetime."

"All right, enough of this sentimental stuff," Brad said, interrupting. "Goodbye, Nick and Abby."

Nick smiled at his brother. "We're going. You have half an hour before the kids go to bed. And you have to put them in bed. That's your payment for having some privacy."

"You've got a deal," Brad said, holding on to Sarah.

When the door closed behind his brother and sister-in-law, he kissed Sarah several times. Suddenly he released her.

"What's wrong?" Sarah asked.

"I've made a mistake."

"You—you don't think—"

One look at her face and he knew she misunderstood. "No, Sarah, don't pull away. I mean— Well, I think I overestimated my control. I can't keep kissing you and not— You know."

"You haven't changed your mind?"

"No, sweetheart, I haven't, but I'm not

sure what to do now. Because I can't keep kissing you without things getting out of hand."

"Brad, shouldn't we talk?"

"About what?"

"Our getting married. I mean, we haven't talked about it."

"We've been talking about it ever since we got back from Denver. I'm the one who held you after you shot that man. I'm the one who held you in my arms after you delivered the babies. I've been loving you every step of the way. I just couldn't tell you until tonight."

"Oh, Brad, I love you so much."

"And I love you, too. We're going to have a great family—you, me, Anna and Davy."

"Can we tell them?"

"Sure, why not? Of course I think Davy and Robbie might get too excited about it, but we'll be stern."

She grinned at him. "Okay, you be the stern one and I'll be the excited one."

"I like that, sweetheart. Let's go tell our family."

* * * * *

The Colton family is back!
Enjoy a sneak preview of
COLTON'S SECRET SERVICE
by Marie Ferrarella,
part of
THE COLTONS: FAMILY FIRST
miniseries.

Available from Silhouette Romantic
Suspense in September 2008.

He cautioned himself to be leery. He was human and he'd been conned before. But never by anyone nearly so attractive. Never by anyone he'd felt so attracted to.

In her defense, Nick supposed that Georgie could actually be telling him the truth. That she was a victim in all this. He had his people back in California checking her out, to make sure she was who she said she was and had, as she claimed, not even been near a computer but on the road these last few months that the threats had been made.

In the meantime, he was doing his own checking out. Up close and exceedingly personal. So personal he could feel his blood stirring.

It had been a long time since he'd thought of himself as anything other than a law enforcement agent of one type or other. But Georgeann Grady made him remember that beneath the oaths he had taken and his devotion to duty, there beat the heart of a man.

A man who'd been far too long without the touch of a woman.

He watched as the light from the fireplace caressed the outline of Georgie's small, trim, jean-clad body as she moved about the rustic living room that could have easily come off the set of a Hollywood Western. Except that it was genuine.

As genuine as she claimed to be?

Something inside of him hoped so.

He wasn't supposed to be taking sides. His only interest in being here was to guarantee Senator Joe Colton's safety as the latter continued to make his bid for the presidency. Everything else was supposed to be secondary, but, Nick had to silently admit, that was just a wee bit hard to remember right now.

Earlier, before she'd put her precocious handful of a daughter to bed, Georgie had fed his appetite by whipping up some kind of a delicious concoction out of the vegetables she'd pulled from her garden. Vegetables that, by all rights, should have been withered and dried. She'd mentioned that a friend came by on occasion to weed and tend it. Still, it surprised him that somehow she'd managed to make something mouthwatering out of it.

Almost as mouthwatering as she looked to him right at this moment.

Again, he was reminded of the appetite that hadn't been fed, hadn't been satisfied.

And wasn't going to be, Nick sternly told himself. At least not now. Maybe later, when things took on a more definite shape and all the questions in his head were answered to his satisfaction, there would be time to explore this feeling. This woman. But not now.

Damn it.

"Sorry about the lack of light," Georgie said, breaking into his train of thought as she turned around to face him. If she noticed the way he was looking at her, she gave no indication. "But I don't see a point in paying for electricity if I'm not going to be here. Besides, Emmie really enjoys camping out. She likes roughing it."

"And you?" Nick asked, moving closer to her, so close that a whisper would have trouble fitting in. "What do you like?"

The very breath stopped in Georgie's throat as she looked up at him.

"I think you've got a fair shot of guessing that one," she told him softly.

* * * * *

Be sure to look for
*COLTON'S SECRET SERVICE and the
other following titles from*
THE COLTONS: FAMILY FIRST
miniseries:
RANCHER'S REDEMPTION
by Beth Cornelison
THE SHERIFF'S AMNESIAC BRIDE
by Linda Conrad
SOLDIER'S SECRET CHILD
by Caridad Piñeiro
BABY'S WATCH by Justine Davis
A HERO OF HER OWN
by Carla Cassidy

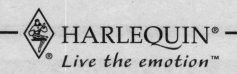

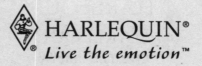

HARLEQUIN®
INTRIGUE®

BREATHTAKING ROMANTIC SUSPENSE

Shared dangers and passions lead to electrifying romance and heart-stopping suspense!

Every month, you'll meet six new heroes who are guaranteed to make your spine tingle and your pulse pound. With them you'll enter into the exciting world of Harlequin Intrigue— where your life is on the line and so is your heart!

THAT'S INTRIGUE—
ROMANTIC SUSPENSE
AT ITS BEST!

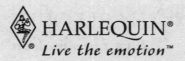

HARLEQUIN®
Live the emotion™

HARLEQUIN®
Super Romance®

...there's more to the story!

Superromance.

A *big* satisfying read about unforgettable characters. Each month we offer *six* very different stories that range from family drama to adventure and mystery, from highly emotional stories to romantic comedies—and much more! Stories about people you'll believe in and care about. Stories too compelling to put down....

Our authors are among today's *best* romance writers. You'll find familiar names and talented newcomers. Many of them are award winners— and you'll see why!

If you want the biggest and best in romance fiction, you'll get it from Superromance!

Exciting, Emotional, Unexpected...

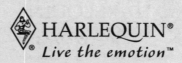

HARLEQUIN®
Live the emotion™

HSDIR06

HARLEQUIN®
Presents®

The world's bestselling romance series...
The series that brings you your favorite authors,
month after month:

Helen Bianchin...Emma Darcy
Lynne Graham...Penny Jordan
Miranda Lee...Sandra Marton
Anne Mather...Carole Mortimer
Melanie Milburne...Michelle Reid

and many more talented authors!

Wealthy, powerful, gorgeous men...
Women who have feelings just like your own...
The stories you love, set in exotic, glamorous locations...

Seduction and Passion Guaranteed!

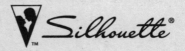

SPECIAL EDITION™

Emotional, compelling stories that capture the intensity of
living, loving and creating a family in today's world.

Modern, passionate reads that are powerful and provocative.

nocturne

Dramatic and sensual tales of paranormal romance.

Romances that are sparked by danger and fueled by passion.